WITHDR

INSTANT LOVE

INSTANT LOVE

[FICTION]

JAMI ATTENBERG

Shaye Areheart Books
NEW YORK

Shaye Areheart Books and colophon are trademarks of Random House, Inc.

Library of Congress Cataloging-in-Publication Data

Attenberg, Jami.
Instant love : fiction / Jami Attenberg.—1st ed.
1. Love stories, American.   2. Loneliness—Fiction.   I. Title.
PS3601.T784I57   2006
813'.6—dc22   2005022743

ISBN-13: 978-0-307-33782-5
ISBN-10: 0-307-33782-0

Printed in the United States of America

Design by Lynne Amft

10 9 8 7 6 5 4 3 2 1

First Edition

Contents

INSTANT LOVE

THE PERFECT TRIANGLE

Holly is getting her makeup done by the burnout girl she befriended at work. They're in the bathroom at the back of the pharmacy, and Shelly's dusting one perfect pastel-colored triangle on each eyelid. Same as hers. She's been staring at Shelly for two nights a week, 5:00–9:00 PM, most of senior year, and has fallen deeply in love with her makeup.

Holly has tried to make the same perfect triangles herself at home, usually with *Seventeen* magazine spread out next to her on the bathroom counter. She looks at the photos and diagrams and memorizes the quick tips, muttering directions under her breath as she stares into the mirror, but it's no use. Her eyes end up looking more like Picasso's than Madonna's. It turns out she's no good at blending in the makeup. She's going to suck at blending in for the rest of her life.

Tonight she's going on a date, that's why all the makeupping. She's going out with a boy named Christian who is nineteen and who likes the Smiths and the Cure and New Order. Holly is seventeen and likes New Order and Echo and the Bunnymen and Joy Division. She knows she should like the Smiths, but

Morrissey seems like such a whiny turd. Holly has lied to Christian about this, because he *worships* Morrissey. Morrissey changed his life forever, that's what Christian says. He's a vegetarian now and everything. Meat *is* murder, he says.

Shelly likes Aerosmith and Judas Priest.

That's how Holly and Christian met, because of music. They were both wearing the same New Order T-shirt, the one with the *Brotherhood* album cover (which is a *classic,* even though it is only a few years old), when Christian came in the pharmacy to pick up his father's heart medicine. No one else wears those shirts in her hometown. Holly lives in a town so small she can barely breathe. That's the joke, she's heard it said before: If you want to breathe, go to the next town over.

Coincidentally, that's where they sell New Order T-shirts, too, in the next town over. At that little shitty record store in the minimall, between the 7-Eleven and the dry cleaner's. That's where they both got their shirts. They talked about that record store for five minutes, how it was such a rip-off but it was the only place around. A line built up behind him, and she thought he was going to leave, but then he stepped to the side and waited, and her heart fucking flung at her chest, hard and fast and repeatedly, because oh my god, *this guy is going to like me.*

No one ever likes her like that.

Because of their age difference, Holly and Christian are keeping their romance a secret. No one wants anyone getting arrested for statutory anything.

Plus the engine on his car is so loud she can hear him coming from a block away, and she jokes about it with him, but she's not kidding, that car is a piece of shit.

And he has shaved the sides of his head and left the hair on top long so that it spills over his narrow face in an awkward way and makes him look vaguely like a celery stick.

Also, there is the matter of Christian living in his father's basement because he doesn't feel like getting a job while half-heartedly taking community-college classes in accounting because he doesn't feel like going away to college. He doesn't feel like doing much of anything except riding around in his car and running errands for his dad, talking about Morrissey, and drinking beer from cans in paper sacks. Holly is two years younger than him, and already she knows she is going to blow him away in life, though she's not sure if she's allowed to feel that way yet, so she beats herself up for being a big snob. She is no better than her girlfriends, who say things like, "Like I would date a guy who wasn't in National Honor Society" because all of her friends are smart-girl snobs.

That's why she likes this burnout girl so much. Shelly thinks it's normal to date a guy who goes to community college. Shelly thinks it's OK to spend an hour putting on eye makeup. It doesn't matter to Shelly if he smokes or drives a crappy car. He has a car, *chica*! (Shelly likes to translate words into Spanish whenever possible. It's the only class she isn't failing.) At least he has a car. At least you have a boyfriend.

SHELLY HAS A SECRET that isn't much of a secret at all. When she was ten, a neighbor kidnapped her and kept her in his basement for ten days. He was fat, with a belly like a pregnant woman's, and he had a wandering eye. Holly remembers when it happened, because it was the first time she was aware of something bad happening to another kid her age. Sure, there had been divorced parents (like hers), skinned knees and broken arms, and Holly even knew a girl whose dog had died after getting hit by the FedEx truck. But no one she knew had got kidnapped and— she was guessing, everyone was guessing, but no one knew for sure except for the police and Shelly's parents—raped by some psycho nutjob who got away with it for as long as he did because he was a regular churchgoer, and no one ever suspects a man who is one with God.

That's what Holly's mother said when they finally busted him. She slapped down the newspaper on the kitchen table, three cups of coffee into the morning, and yelled, "Anyone could see the man was crazy! Look at that eye! You wear one little crucifix around your neck and your shit don't stink."

Holly's mother is a godless heathen. She says this proudly to her two friends in town, who are also divorced and also mothers. They spend a lot of time in the next town over.

She has thin black hair and is tiny and focused, like a firecracker right before it explodes. She is *always* suing Holly's father for more child support. Every time he writes another book, she asks for more money. Holly has a younger sister, Maggie, who has lots of medical bills. Neurologists. Therapists. Pharmacists. "Plus they are two teenage girls, Bill," her mother would say into the phone. "They eat, they shop, they breathe." *The expenses,* her mother hisses.

Holly's mother exhausts her.

Shelly moved away a few months after the trial. She went to live on the other side of the state with her dad, who blamed her mom for what happened. Her mother also blamed herself for what happened, because she was at work, and not at home waiting for her child. And she blamed herself for marrying her husband in the first place. She married him because he was the first one who asked. What if no one else asked? What if? Her life was just one big mistake leading up to her child being kidnapped and molested. So Shelly left and her mother began to drink, and she did this for a few years, she was very good at it, until her boss at the salon told her to cut it out, quit coming to work smelling like you've been making out with Bartles & Jaymes all night long or you're fired. She got herself in a program, went to a lot of meetings, made a lot of apologies, and tried to get her daughter back. A mother should be with her daughter, don't you think?

Shelly always complains when her mom is "twelve-stepping" her again.

Take her, said Shelly's dad. It's my turn for some fun. Shelly's dad throws acid parties now. She sometimes visits him on the weekends and smokes pot with his girlfriend who is only ten years older than her and used to live in Korea and knows how to swear in ten different languages. He's acting like it's the sixties again, that's what Shelly says when she comes back after a visit. He's trying to turn back the hands of time. *El tiempo.*

They are taking turns, this family, with being fucked up. That's what Holly thinks.

Shelly's been back in town for a year, and everyone knows exactly who she is; no one has forgotten a thing. People don't forget things like kidnap and rape and molestation and violation and major jail time in a town so small no one can breathe. No one will touch Shelly. No one wants to go near her, except for the other burnout girls. They recognize her as the kind of girl who has a particular understanding of extreme sorrows inflicted by a different kind of fate than applied to the rest of the world.

It's funny, though, because Holly can see how easily Shelly could be something else besides a burnout girl. All the rest of them have a raw look, narrow and paranoid in the eyes, and they're too skinny (except for the one who is too fat), and have bad skin and wear too much makeup that they've probably shoplifted. Whenever Holly walks by them when they are smoking in the school parking lot, they are always laughing dark, bitter laughs, raw and scratchy and pained. They sound as if they've stayed up late the night before, when she was in bed by eleven, just as her mother asked her to be.

But with Shelly, Holly sees puffy soft cheeks, and pink sad

lips, and otherworldly gray eyes that are always drifting off toward the sky, toward somewhere else besides the fluorescent peak of the pharmacy. Shelly is soft feathered hair, a real natural blond, dirty blond maybe, but blond nonetheless, and perfect pink-and-purple eyelids, and tight black jeans and a form-fitting black button-down flannel shirt that just hits the waist, and high-heeled black boots with a strap and silver buckle around each ankle. Shelly is quiet until you get to know her, and then she has something to say. Shelly has a secret, that's what Holly thinks. When you look at her, you know she has a little secret just bursting to get out of her.

In other words, she's a real knockout.

HOLLY SITS on the toilet seat while Shelly finishes her eyes, and stares at the reflection of the bathroom in the mirror. There are so many signs in this bathroom, reminders of how to be a normal person when you're away from home: Wash your hands. Don't flush sanitary napkins. Please put the seat down when you're done—yes, that means you, Alan, Greg, Schneider, and Mario. ("Please" is underlined, and someone has drawn a star next to it.) There is also a framed print of a sketch of a rose over the toilet. A bottle of air-freshener spray rests on the toilet tank. Lilies of the Valley. What valley?

Shelly tells her to look up, and doses her lashes with mascara. Then she asks if she's in love with Christian.

So are you totally in love with him, Holly?

Christian? Christian who doesn't like to read anything but *NME*? Christian who has things like "Buy Jelly" written on his hand?

Holly laughs as if to say, *As if,* and Shelly looks at her all soft and puffy and sad, like, How can you not be in love? Don't you know how lucky you are? And a little bit of: Then why have I spent the last hour doing your makeup if you're not even in love?

So Holly says, No? Maybe?

Finally she lands on: Well, it's only been five weeks. Which should have been her answer in the first place.

Shelly tells her to stop squirming or you'll fuck it all up. While she leans over she sticks the round edge of her tongue out between her lips and holds it there. Some of the pink eye shadow drifts down from Holly's lid and her applicator onto Holly's chest.

Sit still, she says. Do you want to look hot or not?

HOLLY HATES MAKEUP on principle. Makeup is what other girls wear, girls who need to wear it in order to get attention, or to make themselves feel better, or to feel like they fit in with everyone else. These are girls who cannot carry their weight in the world otherwise. But I am an exceptional person, this is what Holly tells herself in between beating herself up for being such a snobby smart-girl bitch. (She cannot help it if she is the smartest girl, possibly the smartest person, in her AP biology class, and maybe even AP chemistry, too.) She has other things to worry about besides makeup.

Her mother doesn't wear makeup. When Holly asked her once to show her how to put some on, she said, "Really?" and Holly knew her mother thought that that was the dumbest thing she had ever heard. Like, why would you want to? Like, what is wrong with you?

And the truth is, Holly looks better without it. Makeup makes her look darker and older, like she has something to cover up when in reality she has fine, rosy skin, bright eyes with dark lashes, and plump red lips. She is bursting with youth. She doesn't realize it now, but she will in ten years when she looks back at her high-school graduation pictures. She is a ripe plum waiting to be plucked.

But if she's going to have a friend who is a burnout girl, and she's going to date a guy with no future who sometimes wears eyeliner on their dates, if she's going to lead this secret, opposite-world life, she might as well try wearing a little makeup.

EVERY TIME she goes out with Christian, she lets him do something new to her body. She is conducting an experiment. She is her own science project. Mix a hand with the space between the thighs, it feels this way. Apply a tongue to a nipple, it feels that way. Oxygen and water and heat equal steam.

This seems to be the main purpose of their dates, this getting to the half-naked-on-the-black-leather-couch-in-his-father's-basement part of it. The couch impresses her. It has a few cigarette burns on it, but otherwise it's luxurious. All the furniture in Holly's house is wicker or velour or some sort of flower-patterned fabric. The couch totally works on her. All she wants to do is lie on that couch and make out with Christian.

They both have become better kissers in the last five weeks, although he still likes to do this tongue-swordplay action that she thinks requires too much effort for the end result. When she kisses his neck instead, he says: Are you trying to seduce me?

Which is preposterous. She has no idea what she is doing. But she says yes.

And then he says: Are you turned on?

He asks her questions like this, and she has to answer yes even if she feels stupid saying it, because if she doesn't he will stop with the experimenting.

BECAUSE HOLLY is the smart girl who works after school (Shelly is the cute girl who works after school), her bosses have trained her well and given her important responsibilities. She is asked to count pills, balance the register at the end of the night, and look up prescription histories on the computer. She can search by name or address or type of medication, so one day she did a search for the pill and now she knows everyone who is on the pill in her high school. There were surprises. She told her girlfriends some of their names, and now they all giggle and feel superior when they see them at lunch. But also she thinks: Why are they having sex and not me? None of her girlfriends are on the pill. Neither is Holly. Shelly is on the pill, but she says she takes it just to help her cramps and Holly believes her, because Shelly is always sad because she doesn't have a boyfriend.

Shelly runs the lottery machine and video rentals. If someone returns a video late, she pockets the fee and buys scratch-off lottery tickets with it. She splits them with Holly, and the two of them play them at the end of the night when the store is mostly empty. Once Holly won fifty dollars and they both went to Taco Bell after work and got nine million steak tacos and ate them till they wanted to puke.

Holly loves her pharmacy life. She even thought about going to pharmacy school. She's awesome at math and science and it seems like such a relaxed job. But when she told her father about it he said, "Really?" in such a dry, bored tone that she dropped it. Her father is a famous writer and doesn't understand anymore what it's like to be not famous. And even though in her mother's house he is Enemy Number One, Holly would hate for him to find her boring, so she drops the pharmacy dream and thinks pre-med instead.

Sometimes she sees her father on the news or on a talk show, discussing a new book or being an expert on something, and he looks so handsome and confident that she can almost forget he is probably *covered* in makeup at that moment.

—————

CHRISTIAN HAS NEVER even heard of her father.

SHELLY IS DONE. "Perfecto!" she says. She backs out of the bathroom to give Holly more mirror space. Holly leans in, knocks a box of Kleenex into the sink. They're on special this week. She leaves it there. Instead she focuses deeply on the glowing lavender triangles that lie nestled in a base of delicate pink eyelids. I look like I should be going to a party where a band is playing, she thinks. I look dreamy, yet glamorous. I look so fucking hot.

And then Shelly leans in next to her, and Holly sees how they match in the mirror. And how the pink and purple complement Shelly's naturally honeycomb-tan skin, and how the gray in her eyes makes it all look a little risky even, but it totally works. Those eyes take her into the future.

Holly will see girls like her years later when she has finally moved to New York, when she and her friends from college will dress themselves up in revealing shirts and travel downtown on Friday nights to edgy bars in edgy neighborhoods in search of edgy men to take them home. The girl will be behind the bar. Her eye makeup will be perfect, and she will be wearing a halter top that Holly could only *imagine* owning, and when she asks the bartender where she got it, she will say, "My friend's a designer. He made it for me. Isn't it great?"

And Holly will want to be her, just as she wants to be Shelly now, because as soon as she has seen Shelly in the mirror, she realizes that she does not look hot. The colors are all wrong for Holly; on her eyes they're garish, and they make her skin look sallow. On Holly's eyes, the triangles don't look mystical or Middle Eastern; they look like children's blocks. She's not spiritual or ethereal; she's a girl who is wearing too much makeup.

Some girls are made for makeup, some aren't.

She can't take it off, of course. She can't insult sweet, scarred Shelly. Plus Holly was thinking of having her come over to her house sometime and make her up some more. Shelly would lean over her, breath close, in her upstairs bathroom or maybe her bedroom. They could have a sleepover or something when her mom is out of town.

Holly is stuck with this clown makeup for the rest of the night.

CHRISTIAN IS LATE picking up Holly. Christian is always late picking up Holly. Usually she meets him at the Taco Bell after school, on nights she doesn't have to work. She sits on the picnic bench and does some homework and tries to look casual, like she doesn't have a secret. (If she could somehow work it out that people knew she had a secret, without actually knowing what that secret *was*, that would be perfect, but she doesn't think it works that way.) Eventually Christian picks her up in the parking lot and apologizes for being late and blames it on his dad, because it is always his dad's fault.

Everything is his dad's fault, except when it is his mother's fault, Holly has learned. His dad is too old, his dad is too sick, his dad won't ante up with the cash. His mother isn't even worth talking about, except when he is really drunk. A few months ago she kicked him out of her house, three towns over. She doesn't love him anymore. That's all he'll say.

She met his father once. He was in a wheelchair, and he seemed so excited to meet her. He shook her hand and grabbed her wrist and held it. It only freaked her out a little bit.

When Christian is done blaming his dad, they drive through the drive-through and get Nachos BellGrande and a bunch of tacos and two Pepsis, and then they go to his house and eat it and then make out with their awful taco breath. Sometimes they drink beer and then they have beer breath. Tonight he has promised vodka, but that doesn't really taste like anything at all.

She stands and waits with Shelly, both of them behind the counter with their matching eyelids and skimpy T-shirts and armpits deodorized within an inch of their lives. Shelly has never met him. Shelly wants to see him. Shelly wants to know who her secret boyfriend is. How exciting! A secret boyfriend. Everyone in the store is almost ready to leave: the pharmacist, Christine, who has a one-year-old and an unemployed load of a husband waiting for her at home; the stockboy, Mario, who always wears red shirts and black pants and has a unibrow; and the delivery

guy, Schneider, who is probably too old to be a delivery guy—
he's well into his thirties—but Holly couldn't imagine him doing
anything else, the way he shuffles and sneers and seems completely devoid of any math skills. More than any of the other
employees, he's the one who consistently stares at Shelly's ass.

They all want to go home, and she is standing there, waiting, like a jackass.

Christian walks into the pharmacy, straight to the back
counter where Holly and Shelly are standing. He is wearing a black
sweater with holes in both elbows and camouflage pants with ties
at the bottom and huge pockets at the thighs. His hair is slicked
back—He's fresh out of the shower, she thinks. He showered!
For our date!—so she sees the shaved sides of his head. He is one
perfect smooth person now. A tiny cross earring dangles from his
right ear. Forgotten is the tardiness, forgotten is the trashiness,
forgotten are the constant complaints. She is suddenly swooning
with pride that this is her boyfriend.

He looks at her and smiles, and he looks at Shelly and stops.

"You have the same . . ." He motions with his finger at his
eyes. He keeps looking at her. "It looks nice," he says. He is still
looking at Shelly.

"Thanks," Holly says. Over here, she thinks. I am over here.

She introduces them, pauses for a breath, and then she says,
We've got to go, no really, we're late as it is. Late for what? He is
still staring at Shelly. Holly hustles him out the door.

I've got to move fast is all she is thinking.

WHEN HOLLY LOOKS back as she leaves, she sees Shelly is staring at her, and she waves. Shelly does not wave back because she does not see Holly wave because she is staring at Christian.

IN THE BASEMENT, in the basement, with the vodka and the kissing, Holly is urgent and pushy. She drinks two vodka and cranberries in a half hour. She takes off her bra in the bathroom and shoves it in her purse. Then she says screw it, and takes off her underpants, too. She can barely look at herself in the mirror, but she puts on more lipstick.

When she returns he is lying on the black leather couch. Come here baby, he says. She joins him. She starts to lie next to him, but then she moves on top of him. He puts his hands on her ass. She sits up, straddles him, and he puts his hands on her waist and then moves them up to the undersides of her breasts, first outside her shirt, and then underneath it.

Hands combined flat on nipples plus two vodka and cranberries equals a deeper, faster breath.

You're definitely trying to seduce me, he says.

Yes, she says. Yes, I am.

HE HAS HIS hands down there afterward, where Holly has shaved her hair into an upside-down triangle. She shaved it that way because she is a math geek and she likes things to be neat and tidy and have forty-five-degree angles. He forms a "V" with the index and middle fingers on his right hand and tops it with the index finger of his left hand, then frames her triangle and peers through.

"Your bush is sexy," he says. Your bush.

LATER: "So that girl you work with seems really cool."

"You only met her for a minute. How could you tell?" She snaps at him like a trap around an animal's foot. She has just been lying there waiting for this.

"She just did. I'm sorry. You're the one who's always talking about her."

"She's cool, yes." Miserably.

SHE IS LEARNING that people get sick of each other very quickly.

THE NEXT DAY Christian and Shelly hang out at Taco Bell. Holly knows they hang out at Taco Bell because she hears about it from Shelly a week later, as they start their shift together, the two of them straightening their pharmacy smocks, cuffing the sleeves, buttoning the oversized buttons. Shelly's gray eyes are lit up with the exuberance that comes with a new friendship as she tells Holly the details: how he had to rush a new prescription for his father who was so sick, she didn't realize how sick he was—did you, Holly?—how it was right around her break, so they figured it might be cool to hang out, get to know each other, her boyfriend and her best friend from work; and how all they did was talk about her the whole time, how smart she is, how great it is that you're going to be a doctor, how much we'll both miss you when you go away to college in the fall.

Isn't that awesome? That your boyfriend and your best friend from work are friends now? And you know, neither one of us knows a lot of people, both of us are so new in town. So like, how great is it that we each have a new friend?

It was true, Shelly didn't have a lot of friends, and neither did Christian. With their troubled pasts and their bad reputations and their unremarkable academic records. How could she argue with that?

HE HAS KNOWN about it for days, of course, and never mentioned it.

ON THEIR NEXT shift together, Shelly shows up late, with two round red hickeys suctioned on her neck. She passes Holly, fast, and heads straight to the back bathroom, but the bruises are unmistakable. She's probably putting concealer on them, thinks Holly. She had done so herself just two weeks before.

Holly counts out fourteen penicillin tablets for Mrs. Packer, who is leaning against the counter near the echinacea display.

She is gabby, Mrs. Packer. Her daughter Mindy got sick over the weekend. She tells this to the store at large.

"It started with a little cough Saturday morning," says Mrs. Packer, "and by Sunday afternoon she could barely speak. She's going to miss auditions for the school play." Mrs. Packer shakes her head grimly, as if Mindy were about to lose a limb.

Shelly ducks through the storeroom door and slides past Holly toward her post in front of the lottery machine.

"They're doing *Oklahoma!* this year. Mindy wanted to play Ado Annie," Mrs. Packer says.

"The slut," says Holly.

Mrs. Packer says, "What?" It only works for Mrs. Packer if she's the only one talking.

"Ado Annie," says Holly. "She's the slut, right?"

"Yes, I suppose she is, although that's not exactly the word I would use."

"That's the word I would use," says Holly.

SO THIS ONE I don't get to keep, she thinks.

LATER WHEN THEY go to Taco Bell on break, Shelly orders a bean burrito instead of her usual steak taco. "I'm trying vegetarianism now," announces Shelly when the counter guy tries to ring up her regular order.

Holly doesn't question it. Holly doesn't even want to know. "Really?" she says. Holly has no idea what it sounds like when it comes out of her mouth; she only knows the conversation ends immediately.

LOOK, WHAT were you going to do with him anyway? Marry him?

A FEW WEEKS LATER, there is a summit of sorts, held on a picnic bench in a small park near the junior-high school. Christian has lured Holly there with the promise of a picnic, but when she arrives he is seated only with a beer wrapped in paper, and a pack of Camel Lights, the top of the box half-cocked, one cigarette jutting out from the rest. She joins him on the bench, and they sit for a while, space between them, and quietly watch two young girls, identical sisters in matching athletic shirts and shorts, race up and down the wide expanse of grass. They are trying to best each other with a soccer ball. Their hair is long and red and unruly, held back barely with barrettes and ponytail holders. Their cheeks are flushed. There are freckles on their arms. They are wearing training bras masquerading as sports bras. They are fierce. When one finally breaks loose, the other flies gracefully after her, finally tackling her to the ground. She sits on top of her, laughing, until her sister reaches up and smacks her in the face. The sister on top grabs a fistful of the other's hair, and it is on, they are rolling and pinching and biting and it doesn't seem like it's going to stop, until a woman passing through the park with a baby carriage yells at them to cut it out. They start laughing, the two of them, and roll off each other. They lie on their backs and laugh and laugh and look up at the sky, which on this day is gray and thick with chunky dark clouds.

It could rain at any minute.

"Maybe we should get out of here," says Holly. She rolls her eyes to the sky.

Christian checks his watch. He has a watch? He looks past Holly, past the twins, who are now practicing headstands, and then, finally, he sees what he is looking for, and he smiles a drunken smile, which makes no sense to Holly because it is only two in the afternoon. She turns and sees Shelly approaching, almost running, the points of her high-heeled boots sinking into the grass.

Shelly sits on the far end of the picnic table across from Christian, and she reaches out her hand toward him, lays it flat, waiting for the moment he will reach back for hers. And then she says, "We have something to tell you," in such a dramatic fashion it is instantly clear to Holly that all they have talked about for days and days was this moment, that they have been waiting to utter these words, to feel the simultaneous thrill and guilt race through their bodies like a shot of alcohol at the beginning of the night.

And even though Holly is not surprised, she is still hurt, and sad, because now she's going to have to be a complete bitch to them.

HELLO, MA'AM, this is Shelly's friend from work, Holly Stoner, and I don't know how to tell you this, but I thought you should know, I mean *I* would want to know, considering what's happened to her in the past with that man, yes, ma'am, I know it was a long time ago, I know that's none of my business, but what's happening now, like, I'm her friend, so I think maybe it is my business? Anyway, look, she's dating someone, he's older, like, not in high school anymore, over eighteen, yes, definitely, anyway, *they're doing it,* ma'am. And technically, that is rape, you know? He's raping her. I don't think it's right, do you?

SHELLY DOESN'T TALK to Holly anymore after her totally unforgivable act of betrayal. (That's what it said on the note that she slipped in Holly's locker.) Also, she wears his New Order T-shirt with the hole in the sleeve every day to work for a month. It smells like cigarettes. She leans against the lottery machine, perfectly lined eyes staring out toward the birthday-card carousel, and fingers the bottom of the shirt, the ratty cuffs of the sleeves, and the jagged cigarette-burn hole. She is dreaming of her eighteenth birthday.

Like I care, thinks Holly. She has already packed up her shirt in the closet. She likes Sonic Youth now, and the Pixies, bands that have girls who are messy and tough. She is sick of faggy boys who strum their guitars and cry and people who work beneath their potential. She is so over it. In a year she will be somewhere new, studying to be a doctor, a hero, a rock star, and they will still be there, smoking their goddamn cigarettes and eating their stupid vegetarian burritos. In a way I feel sorry for them, she thinks. In a way.

At night she scrubs her face, until her skin is raw and dry and pink, until nothing is left but Holly. She scrubs until it stings.

SARAH LEE
MEETS A MILLIONAIRE

Sarah Lee left Boston in a hurry. There was a pregnancy, and an abortion, and also an arrest. Not of her, but of him, the boyfriend, the one who had gone sour, a crying shame. The boyfriend from high school, from freshman year to senior year, who had taken her under his denim-jacket-clad arm, the jacket with the cigarette-pack outline worn through the right pocket, a patch of a pot leaf sewn on the shoulder. Under that jacket arm she stayed for four years, as he nurtured and loved her, and didn't care if she stuttered, and stared down her three older brothers when they were being dicks to her (and they were always being dicks to her), and looked at all her drawings and told her she was brilliant, that's some great stuff, draw me again, will you, babe? That one, the kind one, with the early stubble, who went on tour one summer with the Dead (Sarah Lee was fiercely and resolutely denied that option by her mother), and when he came back he started buying and selling large quantities of pot, and mushrooms too, so much so that people started calling him "the Ounce" behind his back, until finally there was simply no other choice for the local police but to bust his ass. The pregnancy was two months before the arrest, the abortion one week afterward (Sarah Lee felt nothing for years about it, until she started therapy, and then she cried for a night and pronounced herself "over it"), and the flight to Seattle to stay in the basement apartment of the house of Cousin Nancy, a nurse in a cancer ward, occurred one week after that.

"Here's what you're going to do," her mother had said to her. "You're going to enroll in community college. I've checked already, you can still sign up through the end of the month. Take art classes or whatever you want, I really don't care, Miss Sarah. Just get involved in something. Idle minds, miss. Idle minds. Also you're going to stop smoking. And you're going to cut your hair. Don't dye it again. It looks atrocious. And you're going to stop wearing those goddamn jeans. You can't even take them with you. In fact, take them off right now."

Sarah Lee stared up at her mother standing there, tidy and pressed and twitching in their kitchen. She didn't know what her mother was going to do next. There had been a flurry of commands in recent weeks; her mother was in emergency mode. Sarah had been letting her run her mouth and waiting to see what stuck. It's funny what sticks.

"This instant, Sarah," she said.

Sarah stood, unbuttoned, unzipped, bent, one leg, then the other. She handed the jeans to her mother. There were holes in the knees. Sarah had drawn a picture of her boyfriend on the back pocket in magic marker. Her mother clenched the jeans, looked as if she were going to rip them in two. Sarah sat back in the chair in her underpants. The plastic cover of the chair felt clammy against her legs.

There was more after that. No contact of any kind with the boyfriend. College applications. And even though she doesn't like church, she's going to church from now on. Every weekend. Plus a job, any job. A new attitude. Get your act together. Pronto.

SARAH LEE SAT at a wide wooden picnic table on the back porch of a stranger's house, trying to figure out what to do next. Though the rain had stopped a few hours before, the wood was still damp, and she could feel her jeans soaking through, but she didn't want to go inside. Outside was where her friend was, and it was good to stick with a friend at a stranger's party; outside was where it smelled good, the flowers in the garden, plus the wood and the rain and the grass smelled rich and sweet together. But outside was also where it was quiet, and she didn't like to meet people in silence—her stutter was more obvious then, and sometimes after that, people stopped listening to her completely. (Which is worse? To have never been acknowledged, or to be discarded? She could never decide.) She had compensated tonight by smoking some pot, which relaxed her, slightly stunned her nervousness.

Earlier her cousin had made her stew. She did this every Friday, invited Sarah upstairs for big bowls of her specialty, a spicy stew with thick chunks of beef and tomatoes, sometimes with sweet carrots and cabbage, whatever looked good at the market. Her cousin wanted to make sure she was getting enough iron. Iron was very important, said Nancy. She had a lot of opinions about what was important: fresh air, exercise, fruits, vegetables, and Democrats. Sarah listened to whatever she had to say, she didn't mind. Sometimes Sarah would tell her about her art classes, or funny stories from her job at the bakery. None of Nancy's work stories were funny—it was almost always about another person dying—so she kept them to a minimum. They dipped hunks of bread Sarah brought from work into the stew, clinked together their glasses of red wine (one a day, also important), they rubbed their bellies at the end of the meal and laughed. Sarah thought Nancy was an all-right lady. A little lonely, but all right.

And then, at the tiny mirror in the bathroom of her basement apartment, Sarah Lee had meticulously applied eyeliner, and admitted to herself that it might be time to get a new boyfriend. She didn't know if her ex had tried to contact her, and she could finally admit she didn't care. He was ruined now, soiled by the stain of getting caught, hustled in handcuffs, fingerprinted, fingers pointing, branded for life as a criminal. You can't wash that off, no matter how hard you try.

So she headed to a party with her coworker Melanie, as a replacement friend for Melanie's best friend, Jemma, who had homework to do. Melanie's new boyfriend, Doug, had invited them. The two had met a week before at the park by the reservoir, during a break between classes. Doug was playing Ultimate

Frisbee, and Melanie was making a bag out of hemp (she was always making something out of hemp) that she planned to sell in the parking lot of a Phish show in Portland the following weekend. Doug had thrown a Frisbee into her head, apologized for throwing a Frisbee into her head, told her he liked her dreadlocks, and then they had totally fallen in love.

"He gives me hickeys on my tummy," said Melanie, as they hovered behind the counter at the bakery, the sweet smell of fresh rhubarb pies swirling around them. "Look." She had pulled up her T-shirt. They were plum-colored and surrounded her belly button, which had a silver bar through it. Sarah thought it looked like a tattoo. And if you were into that sort of thing, it was probably very pretty.

She was trying not to judge. No one judged in Seattle. It wasn't cool to judge. People would think less of you if you did, Melanie had told her this. The whole idea wrapped around in Sarah Lee's head and met itself again at the beginning, this judging of judging. She didn't want to disagree, but hadn't figured out how to agree.

Sarah Lee was just trying to sort out the Seattle bus system. That was for starters. The whole judging thing was way down on the list. Not that she had a list. Some people could think that way, in numbers or bullet points or alphabets, but not Sarah. She thought in circles.

IT WAS AFTER ELEVEN. A car door slammed, and there was a shuffle of feet and then a knock at the front door, which echoed to the backyard through the quiet night air. Two voices, two more guys, Sarah thought. That makes fifteen men. Fifteen is either a lot, or not very many at all.

She dug her thumbnail into the moist wood of the table, traced the shape of a heart. There were three other people seated at the picnic table, all guys. Maybe I should say something, she thought. What do I say? I should have something to say.

Everyone else was inside except for Melanie and her boyfriend, who trampled through the grass, smelling the flowers in the dark. Sarah could hear Melanie laughing, a sweet tinkling laugh that usually made an appearance after she smoked pot.

There was a lot of pot at the party. The interior of the house reeked of it, from the front foyer with the beat-up welcome mat where two long-haired software engineers leaned casually, smoking a joint and catching a breeze through the screen door, to the kitchen with the tile scuffed with mud from the paws of the three dogs who lived in the house. The kitchen was where six employees of two competing software companies sat, at an old oak table, passing around a champion-sized bong. They would smoke several hundred dollars' worth of marijuana that night. Six months later their companies would merge. One company would claim it bought the other. Some people would get promoted while others would remain stagnant. Feelings would be hurt. Two college roommates would stop speaking for a decade until their wives forced them to reconnect at another friend's wedding, and then it was as if they had never parted ways.

Sarah turned to her tablemates and hefted herself upon them. She introduced herself. She got their names. She made eye contact. She pulled her hair out of her face and off her shoulders and pulled it up into a ponytail, and then swung it slightly.

This was a bad move, but she didn't know it. Her hair looked much better down, but no one had ever told her that, even when she had asked. She had dated her boyfriend throughout high school, and he loved her no matter how her hair looked, which is how he always responded to the question. Her girlfriends had always said, "Who cares? You have a boyfriend, so it doesn't even matter."

And now here she was, single, and completely ignorant of the fact that when her hair was up her ears stuck out in an awkward way, and while the rest of her was perfectly lovely, with her moon-shaped face and long, wavy blond hair and pink-blushed cheeks, at that exact moment, with the moonlight breaking through the clouds and outlining the halo of the hair on top of her head and the shape of her ears, she looked like she could have been a circus freak, the Amazing Elephant Girl, one tent over from the Bearded Lady, only one dollar, step right up.

MELANIE DID a cartwheel and slipped in the wet grass. She shrieked. Doug laughed and extended his hand to help her stand.

She pulled him down next to her. He yelled. A light went on in a house down the block.

"We're waking the whole neighborhood," said Doug.

"Everyone will know we're having fun," said Melanie.

"Let them know," said Doug.

"I am having fun!" yelled Melanie.

TWO OF THE three men ignored Sarah. It wasn't because of her ears—although that didn't help—but because they were caught up in planning what they saw as a small revolution, even if it could only be viewed on a computer screen. That left Danny West, a sturdy, dark-haired guy in a baseball cap, who figured: Sure, why not give the girl a little chat? The stutter's kind of sexy, actually. She's the only one around anyway, except for that drunk chick talking to Doug, and I think they're together. Danny had nothing better to do, anyway. He had already contributed his part to the revolution and cashed out early.

Danny West was twenty-four years old and a millionaire. Several times over, in fact, but who's counting?

He could not stop counting.

He asked her if she liked it in Seattle, and she said, "It's different than anywhere else I've lived. It makes me feel like I could be a better person," and he liked that answer a lot. She was full of hope, it seemed. Everyone around him had hopes and dreams, and he had already sold his to a guy older than his father.

He didn't know what to do with himself now.

"And what about you?" asked Sarah. "What do you do?"

"Nothing," Danny said. "I'm a lazy sack of shit is what I am."

The two men sitting next to them stopped talking, and one of them said, "Shut up, dude." The guy laughed like he didn't mean it, but he really fucking hated Danny West sometimes. Here the rest of the guys who went to school with West were working their tails off trying to come up with something genius that would change everything, make them rich, make them famous, and set them up for life in every way imaginable, and West had already done all that, made it look as easy as looking both ways and crossing a street. But then he'd just checked out, gone to Thailand and India and all the other places they could only dream of going if they could just get the time off, and then he came back sometimes and just hung around, showed up at parties and talked shit like that. He had simply ceased to be tolerable.

"Well, I used to do something," said Danny. "I invented some software, I started a company, I sold it, and now I'm rich and won't have to work again for a long time. So I mostly travel now. I just got back from a month in India."

He took a sip from his plastic cup casually. It was a well-practiced sip. What do you say after that? You just sip instead.

SARAH'S EYES widened, and she looked prettier. He was the kind of man who looked "good on paper" as her mother sometimes said. Sarah had always tossed that phrase around in her head when she heard it, let it travel like a curious bird. To be good on paper meant something entirely different to her. It meant a face that would be beautiful to draw, a face with character: deep lines on a forehead fresh from worry, a nose with a bump on it from a skateboarding accident, or ears, slivers like a partial moon or sturdy soup spoons like hers. Now here was someone who had something different, a brilliant story to tell, and a fantastic life to be led.

She took down her hair, played with her elastic. Now she was lovely, and excited by him. And she fell in love with him, or loved him a little bit just at that moment. It had never occurred to her that she might actually meet a rich man who could take care of her. She could suddenly see the future with him so clearly.

There were trips to be taken (India! She hadn't even considered India. It was enough that she had made it to Seattle), and she wouldn't have to work those weekend shifts for extra cash; he could help with little things probably.

She found his plain looks problematic, though (He was to become handsome only as an older man: his soft jaw would harden significantly with determination, and the wisdom he was already striving to achieve would eventually imbue his eyes with an irresistibility), and envisioned how a decent haircut and a little bit of stubble could change everything about him. They could move in together, and she could get out of that basement and into his apartment, which she was certain was spacious and lovely. (In fact, she was wrong. He was a simple man who hated to be wasteful. He lived in a small studio with big windows and a lofted bed, downtown near the water. There wasn't really room for another person. It was a deliberate move.) Sarah Lee was smitten.

Melanie and Doug were slow-dancing on the grass. He was humming to her. He dipped her.

Sarah thought: And she and Danny could dance, too. Did he like to go dancing? Did she like to dance? That's what people in love do.

DANNY SAW HER love, but he'd seen it all before, even though he hadn't been a millionaire that long. At first he was coy about his success when meeting new people ("I'm taking time off from work right now," he would say when they would ask him what he was doing. Or, wryly, "I'm unemployed."), but the truth would eventually tumble out of his mouth as if he were a kid excitedly reporting an A on a spelling test over dinner—"I sold my company and now I'm free." Sometimes it would spill out because he wanted to share his excitement, and other times he knew it was the only way a girl would pay him any attention.

Either way he hated himself when he did it for attention, but he couldn't help it. He had earned those bragging rights. He had given up most of his senior year of college (There was a girl, then, a nice one who was as smart as he was, but she didn't have a killer idea like he did, so she couldn't understand when he began to *prioritize* in a way she found *unempowering* to her and her needs. I'm never dating a psych major again, he had yelled at her, and then found out he had effectively terminated his one opportunity to get laid for the year) to start his company and had turned to speed the last six months before he sold the company, burning himself out, staying up late, all to finish one perfect software application. At the end he was cold, his emotions were like aluminum foil, jagged and shielding him from change, and on the night he met Sarah Lee, he was only starting to return to his former self. Only that self was gone; he would never be the same, now that he was a millionaire.

So when he looked at Sarah Lee, all he saw was a girl with pretty hair and a nice rack, but she had those freakish ears and a sudden greed in her eyes, and that in turn made her seem very, very dull to Danny West. He kept scanning, categorizing, identifying. This is not the woman who is going to help me figure my shit out, he thought. She probably doesn't even know who she is. And then: Maybe she'd be a good lay. His eyes dropped to her breasts again. Maybe. That kind of thinking never went anywhere for Danny, but it was part of the assessment. Everyone needed to be assessed.

SARAH WAS TRYING to think of ways to make the millionaire love her. She could offer him comfort, stroke his arm, or let him put his head in her lap. Maybe she should ask him to dance. Maybe she should make him laugh.

She should say the most ridiculous thing in the world that she could think of at that moment, like: "I want to make you pie." Or: "I like cows better than any other animal because they always seem so happy to be exactly where they are." Or: "I love you, my millionaire."

Oh my god, Mom, I married a millionaire. We went to Las Vegas this weekend and he bought me a big ring and we got married in one of those little chapels and then we slept in the fanciest room I've ever seen because he is a millionaire and can afford whatever he wants. He says I can be an illustrator if I want or not. I don't need to do anything but be his wife. And guess where we're going on our honeymoon? India!

Am I going to need shots?

What about sex? She was good at that. They were actually quite sexually compatible, Sarah and Danny, though she couldn't know it just by looking at him. Things that girls he'd dated in the past had either been unwilling or not ready to do (certain positions, explicit language, and the occasional tryst in public places like coatrooms or bathrooms in fancy restaurants or late at night on a beach) Sarah had been doing since she was in high school. She and her ex-boyfriend started having sex almost immediately, when they were both fifteen, and their high energy and adventurous spirits, often fueled by a wide of array of illegal substances (mostly marijuana, but sometimes acid or mushrooms, hash if they were lucky, but never heroin or coke, that shit was scary), led them down adventurous paths rivaled only by the static-ridden porn Sarah watched late at night while she was babysitting her next-door neighbor's twin daughters.

She would have totally done him any way he liked.

Right now he just wanted to be held.

SHE WOULD HAVE appreciated him, and not just for his money, although it's true that's what drew her to him initially. Even though she wasn't a good student, she always admired people who were. He had drive, and she craved that in her own life. Sarah Lee had the habit of mirroring people around her, and had Danny West been in her life in the past, she would have worked hard in school, she would have made it to the top of her class. (Two years later, though, in the throes of art school, she will at last recognize her own drive. She never needed anyone to inspire her to draw. She was going to do that forever.)

Danny needed to be needed. More than anything he wanted to feel like a man in the most traditional sense of the word, although he would never have uttered those words out loud to anyone, except in some veiled manner in bed. He wasn't sure why he was ashamed of this fact, but he thought a lot of men around him felt the same way. They're all just waiting for some girl who will never arrive, a pretty one with a tinkling laugh, who will cling to their shoulder as if she could not stand without its support. But Danny felt he should have something different, and he spends the rest of his life looking for it. Were it, in fact, a different era entirely, perhaps fifty years previous, when people would marry—and stay married—for relatively small reasons, Sarah Lee could have made him happy for the rest of his life.

In any case he had no use for her today.

Instead, after she said, "Wow, India! That sounds so exciting. You sure do lead an interesting life," he pursed his lips to the left, so that his cheek puffed up slightly, and then sighed. He slapped his hands down on the table, looked to his buddies, nodded at them, and then said, "Right. I'm heading out. Later, guys." He turned his head to her, "Sarah, a pleasure. Sorry we can't chat but . . ."

He didn't bother to finish the sentence. His head was already somewhere else. He got up from the table, thought he heard the word "pie" from behind him—pie, that sounded good—and kept on walking in a straight line.

OVER ON THE GRASS, Melanie and Douglas rolled around on top of each other, wrestling as play.

"You're the funniest girl I've ever met," he said.

"No, *you're* funny," she said.

Eventually they stopped and stretched out on their backs, looking up at the collection of stars in the sky.

"Also, I think you are beautiful," said Douglas.

Melanie reached out and held his hand, and they stayed like that until someone called their names. They both sighed. They were happier than everyone else at the party, and they knew they were inspiring jealousy. All those lonely men, and Sarah Lee, who just got blown off by a millionaire.

HE DIDN'T EVEN hear me. I should run after him. Throw him to the ground. Put my hand down his pants. Bite his ear. Give him honey kisses. Tickle his belly. Feed him pie.

THE SLEEPWALKER

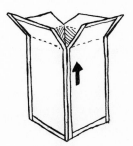

Maggie and Robert were drinking gin and tonics at the patio bar of the most popular restaurant in town. It was their fourth date, and it wasn't going anywhere, at least as far as Maggie was concerned, but she couldn't seem to say no when he called. Robert thought they were taking it nice and slow. Maggie had started drinking more on their dates to make them more interesting, or at least to create a tolerable haze, and Robert kept up with her like a puppy running after its new owner. So while she usually had only two drinks in an evening, Maggie was now on her fourth. Robert had gotten there early to secure a good seat before it got too crowded (This really was *the* place in town, he told her. She was new. She needed his help), so he was on his fifth. And now they were both drunk, she more than he.

"I want to tell you about my day," said Robert. He stopped short of saying, "I want to tell you everything about me."

"So tell me about your day," said Maggie. "That's what I'm here for, to listen. To you. And your day." She ducked her head down. Her auburn hair—thick and soft to the touch—dangled over her shoulders, which were covered, like her cheeks, with freckles. Then she raised her eyes up, opened and closed them slowly, then brushed her cheek against her bare shoulder, like a cat cleaning itself. It was a move that had brought down many men, a move that said nothing at all, yet had the portent of sexuality. She didn't know where she had learned it, only that she had been doing it forever. It had started out maybe as a way to hide, eyes downcast. But then she realized people didn't want her to hide, so she added the upturned eye. I'm still here. I'm in my space, but I'm looking at yours.

OK, that was exhausting, she thought. She pulled her head back, balanced it precariously on her neck, then rested it on the top of her chair and let the last of the setting sun hit her forehead. It made her smile. She thought about taking a nap but decided against it. There should be places where you can nap at bars, she thought. A little nook. A nap nook.

"Well, I was late for work this morning," he said. Robert was practically yelling. It was noisy on the patio, he forgot how loud it could get. If he was trying for romance he had failed, he thought.

"I was getting coffee at this new place over by the convention center—I got a coupon for it in the mail—and when I was walking out . . ."

Maggie watched a waitress serve a woman at the next table a frozen purple drink with a straw shaped like a man's penis, complete with a tiny set of testicles. She had seen the sign for them when she entered. They were called "Purple Pricks," and they were reportedly ideal for bachelorette parties. I would have made the drink blue and called it "Blue Balls," she thought. I should put that in the suggestion box on the way out.

". . . A truck pulls up right next to mine. It's a beater, rusted out, chipped paint, the right front fender was down, you know, a real piece of shit. And this guy gets out. He's only a little younger than me but the way he's dressed—there was something written on his T-shirt, and his hair, like, was so long it hung down in the front?—it makes me think he's a kid."

He sounds kind of sexy, thought Maggie. She missed the scruffy New York boys she used to study at her local bar before she was banished to the suburbs by her employer. (Why didn't it feel more like a promotion? she often wondered.) Those boys wouldn't have dated her—she had always been too clean-cut (*Boring,* she thought. I know what I am) for boys like that—but it made her feel sexier just knowing she was near them. And then she remembered she was on a date. Focus.

"I can see your point," she said. "Bad car, bad hair. Go on."

"So I notice he's pulling stuff out of the trunk. I'm not sticking my nose in his business, but he's just doing it while I'm standing right there, getting my keys out, you know, I had to put the coffee on top of my car, fold up the paper, it takes a while, especially if I"—and with this, he jerked his head back and gave Maggie a playful wink—"haven't had my coffee yet."

"Of course," she said. Robert's fine when he's not being twitchy, she thought. Why does he have to twitch? One minute he's this handsome, normal man with really nice teeth and a lot of money, and the next he's this spazzy kid. Less jerking and whirring and face-making, and more silence. Yes. That would be nice.

"OK, he's pulling out boxes, a couple of boxes of books, it looked like; there were photo albums in there, too, I could see; and then there's two suitcases, old-fashioned ones with leather straps around them, and they're kind of worn. He takes everything out and walks them over to the sidewalk, stacks them up, one by one, next to a bench outside of the 7-Eleven. By now I'm in my car, buckled in, ready to go. You wear your seat belt, don't you? You should always wear your seat belt. I had a cousin who got rear-ended once, and he wasn't wearing his seat belt. Went through the windshield, and now he can't see out of his right eye. He sued the guy, though, and now he never has to work again. I think I'd rather be able to see out of both eyes, though, you know?"

Maggie nodded somberly. She looked to the side and made eye contact with the waitress, motioned for another. "You, too?" she said to Robert, then held up two fingers for the waitress.

"Sure. Why not? It's Friday night and it feels all right, right?" He raised his eyebrows. "Now where was I?"

"7-Eleven."

"Right. So he walks back to the truck, opens the passenger side. There's someone sitting in it; I can't see, I'm too far back, but now I've got to wait and see, right? Turns out it's an old lady. He helps her down, walks her over to the bench, then walks away, no kiss, no wave good-bye, no nothing, just hops back into the truck and pulls away, leaves her right there in front of the 7-Eleven. I watch all the other people walk by, and nobody says a thing."

"Isn't that interesting," said Maggie. What's interesting? Something was. She didn't know what yet.

SINCE THE AGE of five, Maggie had been a sleepwalker. It was possible she had been doing it longer than that, but it was a few days after Maggie's fifth birthday—two slices of pink-frosted birthday cake still left in the refrigerator—that her mother first recalled finding her out of bed, late at night, eyes wide open, standing in the doorway of her parents' bedroom, tiny hands slapping on the already open door as if she were banging some tribal drum. Once they uncovered her disorder, everything changed at once.

"Let's make a list of everything we need to do," said her mother. "To help Maggie." Diane was tiny and seemingly battery-powered; she never stopped running. Her husband, Bill, called her his "secret weapon" sometimes and his "ballbuster" other times.

"You just let me know what I need to do," said Bill. "What I can fit in between classes and writing. Because I will be there. I will do it."

"Bill—"

"You know my schedule," he said. "Work with me here."

So first Diane took Maggie to the doctor, then a specialist, then a sleep-disorder institute; there were tests and pills, and then she sent her to a therapist to see if there was anything traumatic going on there deep underneath, you know, in the subconscious, like some secret that she didn't know about. Diane didn't even want to think about the worst that could have happened. (This was when they first started putting the faces of missing children on the sides of milk cartons, and Diane would study them carefully over breakfast each morning, then keep an eye out wherever she went. This obsession carried on throughout her life; she was proud to have started the first neighborhood watch in their community. When she retired she bought a police radio on the Internet and would happily listen to the local force's regular banter well into the night.)

No, said the first doctor, and the second, and the next and the next. There's nothing wrong with your little Maggie that we can see. She's happy, she's healthy. In fact, what a delight! It's probably just a glitch in the system.

Meanwhile Maggie was an unstoppable night cruiser, and her family's house was her terrain. She found her way into every crevice of the home, from the laundry room to the dank crawl space she wouldn't go near when she was awake, up and down the stairs, into both bathrooms (including in the shower, where her parents once found her sitting in an inch of cold water), her big sister Holly's room quite frequently, and of course her parents' room, where she would sometimes hover over them as they lay hugging opposite sides of the bed, Maggie squeezing and opening her fists and gently counting to ten. She often expressed an affinity for tapping and thumping and pounding, and that's how her parents usually found her: they followed the noise. It was as if the house was haunted, that's how they felt sometimes, only there was no ghost, just a little girl who couldn't sleep through the night.

And while they tried to prevent her mobility with baby guards and locked doors for rooms they considered danger zones, they knew that eventually they would have to find another solution, that she would get taller and stronger and smarter and would be able to take down anything they threw her way. There was also the fear that she would start falling more, down steps, or down anywhere really, and break a limb or hurt her young, fragile head. She already had bruises up and down her knees, so much so that her parents were called into Maggie's school, where they were forced to provide documentation of her illness to an uncomfortable-looking principal and a fiery teacher who had the audacity to imply that they were incompetent parents.

"It's about keeping your eyes open," she said. "Eyes and ears, Mr. and Mrs. Stoner. It's not that hard."

"We're going to move, that'll help," explained Diane to the school principal. "We're going to move to a ranch house—no stairs. And carpeting in every room. It's not because we're not trying, we are. It's just *hard*." Her eyes filled up with gentle tears.

The principal looked at her husband, but Diane didn't bother. She knew he was looking at the bookshelf behind the principal's desk, or at the view of the empty playground through the window, or anywhere at all, really, that took him somewhere else.

AS THE WAITRESS arrived with their next round, Maggie and Robert both drained their drinks, making a sucking sound as the last of the gin-soaked cocktails flew up their straws. Maggie rattled her straw around the ice. The waitress, who was wearing a skimpy terrycloth tank top and shorts and a pin that said, "Ask me about our appetizers!" dipped and swiveled gracefully as she served their drinks. Robert smiled at her and said, "What about 'em?"

"What about what?" said the waitress.

Robert pointed to her chest. "Your appetizers."

"Oh," she said, as if he were the first person to ever respond to that particular call to action, but Maggie knew that couldn't be true, that people probably asked about her appetizers all the time. She's probably drunk, like we are. Maggie had decided, as the noise on the patio heightened with the bellows and cackles of local young singles, that everyone around them was drunk, and that life was comprised solely of periods of sobriety and inebriation, and when you were young and single and, especially, alone in a new town as she was, there were bound to be more periods of inebriation. So she was only abiding by the rules.

". . . Jalapeño poppers, mozzarella sticks, spicy mozzarella sticks, fried cheese bread, and nachos. You can get those nachos with beef, chicken, or vegetarian style. It has a name. Um, Macho Nachos. All of the appetizers have names. You don't need the names, though, do you?"

"How about nachos? With chicken. That'll hit the spot, huh?" said Robert. He leaned back in his chair, crooked his arm over the top of his head, and then slapped his lean belly with the palm of his hand. "We need a little something to take the edge off." He leaned into Maggie as the waitress walked away, and said, voice lowered, "I hope you don't mind me ordering for you. You look like you could use some food. No offense."

"None taken." Maggie looked down at her drink. She didn't want it anymore, but you shouldn't waste a drink, should you? She burped quietly and tasted gin mixed with an acidic flavor.

"Should I . . . ? Yes? All right, well, I couldn't just leave her there without checking on her, could I? The poor woman looked so sad when the truck took off. She pulled all of her boxes close around her. I thought she was going to cry. Hoo boy, that would have been a mess. Grandma's crying out in front of the 7-Eleven again. Anyway I went up to her and asked her if she was doing OK, and she looked up at me with such soft, I don't know, grateful eyes, I damn near melted inside."

A busboy stopped by with place settings for their table. He looked at Maggie, and she gave him a shaky smile. Then she rested her hand on her heart, as if she were about to do the pledge of allegiance. "Thank you," she said to him, with complete sincerity. She ran her fingers over the knife, which was spotted with small bubbles of dishwashing liquid. She stuck her thumb in her mouth, wet it, and then rubbed it on the knife.

Robert watched her. "You all right there, kiddo?"

"I'm fine. I'm just drunk." She looked down at the knife. She rubbed it some more. "I want you to shut up and keep talking."

Robert put his hand on hers and she let him keep it there.

"Turns out she's got a place nearby. She was going to call a cab to help her get the rest of the stuff home, but she was taking a little rest first. She doesn't say who the kid was, where she was coming from, why he didn't just take her home, nothing. I don't know if it was pride or maybe she had a touch of the crazy and it just didn't seem weird to her at all. I got the feeling, though, that if I left her there she might forget to call that cab and just keep on sitting there through the day and night. This little old lady and her boxes."

Boxes, she thought. She remembered something, then—a box from her childhood, and a flash of her mother's voice, panicked. (Her mother was usually either panicked or angry.) And her chest tightened, as if someone had taken a hold of her insides with their hand, finger by finger, until there was a clench of a fist.

THE RANCH HOUSE was grim, and not nearly as spacious as their last home, or at least it felt that way because there was less light. But it was only a few blocks away from their last house, which made it ideal because the girls could stay in the same school, and her parents could use the same sitter, plus it was only fifteen minutes away from the university. They still had three bedrooms, and a living room and a dining room and two baths, but the new study didn't have the towering twin set of built-in bookshelves like the last house, and there wasn't a crawl space, either, which was fine by Diane—those things could be death traps, but that meant less storage space and more clutter. So before they moved, Diane started throwing things away without asking her husband, and when he put up a fight (They spent hours talking about it. *Hours*. Like she didn't have a thousand other things to do with her time. And he wanted to *talk*), together they decided he should rent a storage unit for all his books, the ones that wouldn't fit in whatever new bookshelves they bought, or in his office at school.

Still, despite her best efforts, the day before they moved, their house was filled with boxes. There were the girls' boxes, full of dolls (the new ones and the old favorites she couldn't get them to part with, no matter how much she begged) and board games, their clothes and favorite beach towels, bedtime books, daytime books, records they liked to sing along with while they helped Mommy fold laundry (she usually just had them pair socks, made it into a game to keep them quiet), toiletries and medicine (allergy medicine for Holly and an array of vitamins for Maggie, each one more expensive and useless than the next), and every single art project they'd made since they'd been old enough to pick up paste, glitter, and childproof scissors. And then there were Diane's boxes, which had everything else for the home, from the kitchen and the bathroom and all of the bedrooms, things to cook with and to make you feel comfortable and to keep you healthy. Basically everything you needed to furnish a home she had covered, in her boxes.

Finally there were her husband's boxes; he had insisted on packing his separately ever since he found his collection of Rolling Stones records at the curb in front of their driveway on garbage day. "It's the Stones, for God's sake, Diane! The Stones!" he had moaned. He told her to stay away from his boxes.

To tell the truth, she didn't even want to know what he had packed in them. She was only going to have to contend with them when she unpacked them at the other end. He had done it haphazardly, of course—she noticed when she woke up early the next morning—hadn't even bothered to tape them shut. Diane cursed him silently. The movers were coming at 8:00 AM, and here she was at 6:00 AM, walking around in her bare feet and nightgown, taping boxes shut when he's the one who should be taking care of things like this. A little help, she said to herself. All I am asking for is a little help.

MAGGIE NEEDED a glass of water. Now. She looked desperately around the patio. Their waitress was busy, balancing a pitcher of beer in one hand, a tray full of plates in the other. A busboy helped a band of long-haired musicians carry their equipment to a small stage area on the far side of the patio. She turned to Robert, who was plowing through an obscenely large pile of nachos. Maybe he can help me, thought Maggie. Maybe *that's* what he's there for.

"I really need some water," she said slowly.

Robert's head shot up. "Of course you do. I'm sorry. Hold on." He got up and walked over to the busboy. She watched him motion to the table and then thank the busboy.

"He'll be just a second, honey," he said.

I really don't think he should be calling me "honey," she thought, but instead she said, "Tell me the end of your story. I hope it's a happy ending."

"I don't know if I would call it happy. It's not sad, either. It's more . . ."

"Bittersweet?" said Maggie.

"Something like that," said Robert. "So. I said I'd take her wherever she needed to go, took all of her boxes, put them in the trunk of the ol' Saturn, put the suitcases in the backseat, put the little old lady in the front seat—"

"What was her name?"

"Ann. That's my mom's middle name, actually. Huh. I should have told her that." Robert looked off thoughtfully in the distance for a second.

"What?" said Maggie. "What are you thinking about?"

"Oh, I was just wondering if that band is the same one I've heard here before. They do a lot of Jimmy Buffett covers. Good stuff."

I hate Jimmy Buffett, she thought. She squeezed his hand. More story.

"Anyway, it turns out she lived kind of far away, pretty close to the city, actually, but at this point I'm already going to be late, and I don't know, seize the day, right? It's been so nice out and I've been working so much lately, I just wanted a little time for me. Even if I was helping her, this lady, it sort of also seemed like it would be for me, too. Do you think that's wrong?"

"No, I think that's very, very right," said Maggie. A busboy appeared with two glasses of water. Maggie took a hearty swig from hers.

"Good. So we're in the car, and she's not talking. She tells me her name, where she lives, but doesn't really offer anything else up. It's OK, I didn't need to know, you know? I was just going to get her home, that's all I cared about at that point. After about a half hour, she tells me to turn off, and it's this neighborhood, I've seen it a lot on newscasts. It's not the safest place in the world for an older person, I'll tell you that. She lived in this smallish building, no elevator, and the lobby smelled like piss."

Two tables over a man put his hand on the waitress's hip. She slapped it away.

"I pull out her boxes from the trunk, start walking them up the stairs, to the third floor, where her apartment is. She's dragging a suitcase on the stairs behind me. I didn't like her doing heavy lifting, but she swore it wasn't that heavy. So we get to her place, she unlocks the door, and it's one room. There's nothing in it but a mattress, a television set on the floor, and a chair by the window. No table, no furniture, no telephone, no nothing. All the stuff I have, that I can't live without? Turns out you can live without it."

"I already knew that," said Maggie. Did she?

"Yeah, well, I guess I didn't. Or maybe I knew and forgot. Whatever. I walk her over to the chair, tell her to sit down. I go back down to the car, I get the rest of her stuff, takes me a couple of trips, but I'm in shape, right? I can handle it." He smacked his stomach.

He loves his stomach, thought Maggie.

"I was sweating at the end, though, I'll admit it. She sees this, so she gets me a glass of water. And while I'm standing in the kitchen, she finally says to me, 'My grandson, he's not a bad person. That was just as far as he could take me.' Can you believe that bullshit?"

"No," said Maggie. "I cannot believe that bullshit." Her self-righteousness felt briefly like sobriety. She picked up his glass of water and drank most of it, and when she looked up she realized that everything was suddenly slowing down for her. All the noise around her was so loud that it became quiet. She could now separate everything in her head. Him and her and the rest of them.

"It's not nice, I know that," said Robert. "And I said to her, 'Ann, if you were my grandmother, I wouldn't leave you sitting in front of a 7-Eleven, no matter how busy I was. It's not right, it's not respectful, and you deserve better.' And then I handed her all the money in my wallet and told her to buy some furniture. At least a table so she has something to eat off of. Jesus."

All of the noise and useless thoughts that had crowded her mind in her drunken haze of the past few hours, she had pushed through them all, they were all behind her now. She would have left that old woman sitting there; she probably wouldn't even have seen her in the first place as she walked by, her head in the clouds.

Here she was, staring at someone who had done something she would never do. Robert is the kind of man who takes care of business, a gentleman, a man who not only doesn't abandon people, but also takes them to a better place. He can teach you the right way.

Oh, my god, thought Maggie. He's *good.*

"And then what happened?" Maggie's cheeks were flushed.

"And then I left and went to work. I was almost two hours late. And my boss asked me where I was and I said, 'I had to drive my grandmother to the doctor,' and he said, 'I thought your grandmother was dead,' and I said, 'No, the other grandmother,' and that was that."

"I want you to take me home," said Maggie. "Tonight. I mean, do you want to take me home tonight?"

THERE WERE BOXES everywhere, one stacked on another, filling the living room and spilling into the kitchen. Diane sat on the couch and stared at them. It was her favorite time of day because it was quiet. Her husband was still asleep, he wouldn't get up until just before the movers came; the kids were still nestled in bed, probably having conversations with themselves. It was just Diane and the sum of her material life right now, surrounding her in a sea of cardboard.

There was a shuffle on the steps, heavy, so she knew it was her husband.

"Is there coffee?"

She shot her hand up in the air and wagged her fingers at him. "Five minutes. I just need five more minutes to sit."

"I'll join you," he said, and he sat on the opposite end of the couch. After a moment he said softly, "I liked this house."

"I don't want to hear it," she said. "We didn't have a choice."

"I just wanted to say it out loud."

"Fine. You said it. Now drop it." Diane dug her fingers into her hair and pulled until she could feel her hair tugging at the roots.

"All of this used to be a lot more fun," he said. "I'm exhausted, Di. I mean it."

"Oh, *you're* exhausted." If she weren't so tired, she would have slapped him right then. And she would have made it hurt, too.

He stood. She remained seated.

"I'll make the coffee," he said.

"Great," she said.

As he turned to walk toward the kitchen, one of the boxes began to rock, ever so slightly, but they both saw it. And then they heard a muffled cry. Then, a call for help from their youngest child.

"Oh, my god, she's in the box," said Diane. "Jesus, get the scissors, get the scissors!"

Soon after that morning Professor Stoner started spending more time around the office, and less time at home. Everyone noticed, but no one said a thing.

"THERE'S SOMETHING I need to tell you," said Maggie as they lay next to each other in bed, her leg strapped around his waist.

"You're married," said Robert.

"No."

"You've got a disease."

"No."

"You hate your father."

"Well, yes, that's true, but shut up and listen." She punched his shoulder. "I'm a sleepwalker. I have been since I was a little girl. You should know that. So if you wake up and I'm not around, it's probably because I'm somewhere in the house. I'm much better now, but it still happens sometimes."

"What makes you do it?" he said.

"I don't know. I've been to a million doctors. The last one prescribed sleeping pills, so you can see how that's going. I mean, like I'm going to take pills for the rest of my life?"

Robert made a sad face—exaggerated frown, wrinkled forehead, eyes squeezed close—and she hated him briefly, then beat the feeling down. *If this is going to be the one I love, I better learn to love the sad face.*

"But . . . I can tell you what I see when I do it. It's kind of weird, though. I haven't really told that many people."

"Tell me," said Robert. He was *way* too enthusiastic, she thought. She hoped she wouldn't regret it, any of it.

Maggie took a deep breath. "I'm inside a long tunnel, and at the end is a door, and it's sealed shut. Where I am isn't so bad, but I know that on the other side is a wonderful place, the best place in the world. As I've gotten older, that place has changed, but I always have this feeling like, *I have to get there.* When I was a kid it was either heaven, the picture-book version of it with angels playing harps and clouds and blue skies, or a carnival, where all the rides were empty and I didn't have to wait in any lines and there's as much cotton candy as I want. Then as I got older it became an empty beach during the middle of a hot day, and there's a cooler of everything I want, sandwiches and drinks and chips and, oddly, the most perfect apples in the world, red and juicy, and a beach towel and a radio and an umbrella, just like, the perfect setup for one person. Then it was a carnival again for a while, which was totally strange. I mean, my therapist *loved* that. And these days it's a beautiful park, with kids playing soccer in a field nearby, and an ice-cream man, and a few dogs running around, and I would be walking to meet someone, though I don't know who, if I could just get through that door. So I bang and pound on it, hoping someone will answer it, but no one ever does." She sat up. "And then I wake up. And I'm somewhere in my house, usually the bathroom, but sometimes the kitchen."

"Is it scary?" he said.

"No, it's just frustrating. Because I can never get what I want even though I know it would be so good."

"Well, you won't be sleepwalking on my watch." He wrapped his arms around her. "I'm not letting you go anywhere." He didn't let her go for the entire night. It felt a little uncomfortable, but eventually Maggie got used to it. She did try to get out of bed once, early in the morning, but Robert woke with her and said, "Wake up, Maggie. I'm right here," while she struggled against him until finally they both closed their eyes again, and slept well into the afternoon.

WHAT HAPPENED WITH
WOLFOWITZ

Years ago, Alan was telling me a story about his mother and father and how they fell in love.

OH, ALAN! You of the warm, soft beard and gentle smile and ample cock. You who told me I had a great "tushie," a word so foreign to a woman like me, who was raised by people who said they traded in God for academia. They were so cold, so cerebral, so not fun. Oh, Alan, I still burn with desire for you!

ANYWAY. Alan was telling me a story about his mother and father and how they fell in love, that it was a rocky road, just like the ice cream, but not as sweet.

"Ice cream," I said. "That sounds good."

When I was dating Alan I would eat ice cream every night after dinner, until my hips and belly stretched out and over the top of my jeans. I didn't care one bit. This was when I was in graduate school in Chicago. I had moved there after a few

drunken, poverty-stricken years in New York. I'd had it with trying to find my way drunkenly from the front of a bar to the bathroom, only to return and find my drink gone, my wallet empty,
and the guy I'd been flirting with all night out in front of the bar
making out with someone else. Or worse yet, he would be waiting, the scent of cab fare home mixed with cigarette smoke and
hormones wafting from his body. When a grope in the backseat
of a taxi seems fair trade for a quick ride uptown at 3:00 AM, it's
time to leave town. I had decided I would only return with at
least a master's and some sort of future. So I worked long days in
the lab, roasting my brain slowly over an open spit, and at night
I wanted to treat myself. I liked Alan and I liked ice cream.

I got up and went to the refrigerator, opened the freezer, and
pulled out a pint of my favorite kind, mint–chocolate chip. I like
my ice cream simple, not with cookie dough or M&Ms or
hot sauce or sprinkles. Just cold and sweet with a bit of chocolate in it.

"They met in high school," he told me. "Walter and Naomi,
the most unlikely couple in town. That's what the senior class
voted them—'Least Likely Couple.' And here they are, thirty-
odd years later, still married. Goes to show you what the rest of
those kids knew."

If I heard that today I'd probably reply, "Yeah, and I bet half
of them are divorced now anyway. Or dead."

Instead I said: "They were jealous of their true love, that's all."

"Mom was one of the prettiest girls in school. You should
see pictures of her from then, Holly. Next time you come over,

I'll show you. Dark hair, red lips, a little zaftig but that was more desirable back then. I mean, it's still desirable for me of course." He reached toward me and pinched my rear. "But she was just gorgeous, my mom. Everyone said she looked like Elizabeth Taylor, but Jewish."

I had met his mother once. I didn't see the Elizabeth Taylor resemblance, but I had to admit she was a remarkably manicured woman. Her hair, trimmed short, was dyed the color of a fresh cup of coffee with milk, and lay precisely in place. Her creamy linen suit was tailored and wrinkle-free, as if she had freshly pressed it moments before seeing me. And with an artist's eye she had deeply and intensely outlined and colored her lips with a frosty mocha tint. I pictured her knowing the name of everyone who worked at her salon, whether they cut her hair or not.

Me, I get haircuts so infrequently I can't remember where I got it cut last. Though when I was dating Alan, I started making trips to salons more often. He bought me a gift certificate once for an upscale place near my apartment, which made me think he wanted me to be a more upscale girl.

"Use it for anything you want, sweetheart. Hair color, manicure, waxing. Ask the girls there. They'll help," he said.

I hadn't known I needed help.

I SAT DOWN at the table and spooned some ice cream in my mouth.

"So Mom was a stunner," Alan continued. "But Dad? Not

so much. He was balding before his sixteenth birthday, plus he has that hawk-nose thing. You know what I'm talking about?" Alan outlined an awkward shape with his fingers.

"And his family, they didn't have much money. But Dad was a salesman then, just like now. Sometimes that's all it takes. Talking 'em into it."

"Hey," I said. I tried to muster up a snappy retort, but the ice cream was freezing my brain.

"Not you, Miss Stoner. You're a smart cookie. Plus I don't have to talk you into a thing, you little tramp."

It was true. I was crazy for sex with him, the way he tossed me around so handily, as if I were still just a girl. I was planning on having sex with him as soon as he had finished his story, and I my ice cream. Calling me a tramp only amped up my arousal. Not a lot of people think to call Ph.D. candidates in biology "tramp," but we like it just like everyone else. Not "hussy," though. We hate that.

"So Mom started dating the jeweler's son, Jonathon Wolfowitz. 'Great birthday presents,' she said."

Alan winked at me. My birthday was two weeks away. He had been hinting at something special for a month.

"It's a huge chain now, actually," he said. "You know Wolfowitz and Sons?"

I had seen their ads in the paper since I had moved to Chicago, the most recent one depicting a bejeweled array of Mrs. Wolfowitzes, with their highlighted hair and perfectly lined lips, the younger ones displaying their propped-up cleavage, all beaming saucily at the camera. The tagline underneath the photo read, "It's Either Half Now or Half Later."

"I found a condo for one of their cousins last year," said Alan. "A two-bedroom, great light, an OK view of the lake. Some people, they don't care about the view, they just care about the light."

Alan was a highly successful real-estate agent, and as far as I know, he still is. At the time, he represented a couple of Chicago Bulls, a handful of politicos, and was making headway with a bunch of United Airlines honchos, all seeking something special on Lake Shore Drive.

That was Alan's shtick. "I will find you something special," he would say, in such a way as to make the clients feel that, because they were so special, they simply could not live in anything less than special—that it would be a crime! That's what it's like when you have a lot of money. You can pay people to make you feel good about yourself.

"HE BROUGHT HER home to meet the family, took her to all the school dances, she wore his class ring. The whole nine. His folks even offered to take her to their winter cabin back east for the holidays."

He stopped talking for a moment, loosened the spoon from my hands, and took a bite of ice cream.

"And I remember my mother made a point of saying—I guess it was a big deal—that her family and their family sat next to each other at shul over the high holidays."

"For the whole world to see," I murmured.

"Exactly. A public proclamation. Wolfowitz was a catch. My mother has told me that a million times."

"Why is she still talking about him after all these years?" I said. I meant to say it in my head, and was surprised to hear it come out of my mouth. The public questioning of any and all Naomi actions was a privilege extended solely to Handelman family members. All civilians were required to keep their mouths shut.

"Because he's part of the story, their story," Alan snapped. And then he relented with, "But I know what you mean. I wouldn't want to hear about my competition for the rest of my life."

I nodded. I looked down at my bowl. It was nearly empty. I thought about getting some more ice cream. I decided it could wait. "So let me hear the rest of the story," I said.

"I should have waited for her to tell you," said Alan. "I don't do it justice."

I was in no hurry to meet his parents again. I'm not going to say it was a total disaster, but there was no way I was going to win, looking like I do, which is to say: not Jewish, at least not enough to count anyway. I've got dark curly hair, but my clear blue eyes, Irish and smiling, betray my shiksa identity. That's what his mother called me after she met me. "A very nice shiksa."

Alan thought that was a good thing, the "nice" part anyway.

OH, ALAN, I would have been nice to your mother forever!

"YOU'RE TELLING the story just fine," I said. I patted his hand. "Please. Carry on. I'm interested."

"Do you want some more ice cream?" he said. "Go on, I'll share it with you."

I rose and went to the refrigerator again. You didn't need to tell me twice.

"So the whole time she's going out with Wolfowitz, Dad's trying to steal her away. He always says he loved her from the minute he saw her, and he had no intention of taking no for an answer. He would walk with her down the hallway at school and tease her about, I don't know—her hair, her clothes, general flirty high-school stuff. That was at first. Then he starts saying, 'That Wolfowitz, he's no good. He's got a wandering eye. I saw him sitting with Judy Kanter at lunch, and you know what everyone says about Judy Kanter.'"

Alan had slipped into an impression of his father, neck sunken in toward his shoulders, hands up in the air, torso tensed.

"What did everyone say about Judy Kanter?" I said.

"Dad said she was a real knockout. Big breasts, and this extremely sexy lisp. He knew a couple of guys that got with her senior year."

I mock-gasped, shocked and dainty. "Judy, Judy," I said.

"I know!" said Alan. "But she wasn't that sharp, and say what you will about my mother, she's sharp," he said proudly. "Anyway, he was working on her, always talking, keeping Mom on her toes, like he still does today. 'I was selling,' he said to me. 'I was selling her on me.'"

"Sounds familiar," I said. I sat down next to him and fed him some ice cream. I kissed him on the lips. They tasted cold and minty, but felt soft. I squeezed his generous arm. I kissed him again. "That's what you Handelmans do."

"And we do all right," he said.

ALAN, YOU didn't have to sell me on anything. You were the warmest man I had ever met, the first man that was unafraid to talk about love, although now I know if men offer it up so easy, they're not usually sincere. I didn't care that you were absurdly close to your mother. Or that you frequently went on vacations to Florida without me because they were "family-only" trips. Or that on most weekends, you disappeared into the warm, all-consuming bosom of your parents' home in Highland Park, far, far away from me. What time I had with you I treasured. I loved it, in fact. Even if it wasn't real. Even if it was temporary. Even if I wasn't myself. Because I never got to feel like that again.

HE STARTED unbuttoning my blouse at the kitchen table, kissed my breasts through my bra, then pulled one out and kissed it some more. "It tastes like sugar," he said, and I moaned. I moved onto his lap and he gripped my ass firmly with his hands, then gave it a good slap. "Uch. You," he said.

I kissed his forehead, and then his lips. His soft beard felt nice on my chin, like one hundred tiny scratches. "What happened with Wolfowitz?" I said.

"Screw Wolfowitz," said Alan, and then he took me to bed.

In bed he was like a wolf, all hairy arms and legs, howling at the moon. He pawed at me and held me tight. He held me down, hands on my breasts, and pinched and nuzzled them. He squeezed my hips and ass right before he put his heavy cock in between my legs, and then in me, as deep as he could go. And then he forced me to look at him, not through any words or actions, but through a magnet stare. He locked me, and then I was stuck there, for as long as he liked, in his arms.

This was different for me, this link with another. I had always felt a divide between myself and other men in bed, and it was easy to shut down, look above and around, at anything else but them. (Jesus, he's got a Grateful Dead poster. But we met at a Pavement show. And, oh my, there's a tapestry on the wall. Is it too late to ask him to pull out?)

I could disconnect and reconnect at will. I would check out for as long as it took, let my body warm up from their heat. And then when they were done, I would demand some attention until I was done, too. Bite my nipples until I tell you to stop. Do it harder. All right. Now you can stop.

Alan, however, required attention. Alan wanted ownership.

No problem. He owned me. From the minute we had met—an accident, I walked into the wrong apartment, the expensive one featuring four bedrooms and a balcony with a view and light, light everywhere, that he was showing, not the sullen one-bedroom I eventually took—I liked him, with his grownup suit and his quick mouth and his big, hungry lips. He thought I was someone special, so he showed me around the apartment, and for a little while, I let him believe it because I wanted to keep talking to him. He had me in his clutches, he was thinking, but it was really I who did not want to let him go.

At the end of the tour, after he knew everything about me in ten minutes flat—Single? Right now, yes. Jewish? Sort of, half, once removed on my father's side. A scientist? Yes, you're right, I am a very smart young lady—he asked me what I thought of the apartment.

And then I touched his shoulder and said, "Actually I think I'm lost."

He shook his finger at me, and stretched out his lips, revealing two rows of large, clean white teeth. I bet he had braces forever, I thought. "I had a feeling you weren't looking in the right place," he said.

And then he put his hand on my shoulder, and we stood like that, hands on shoulders, until he asked me out to dinner. Even after I said yes, we still held on for another minute, finally interrupted by a knock at the door, a gasp of air between us, and then the entrance of the next client, a divorce lawyer from Minneapolis who was moving on up in the world, taking his wife and two daughters and leaving the Twin Cities behind for a big Chicago paycheck.

Boy, have I got a view for you.

THE REST OF the Wolfowitz story tumbled out later, when I was lying on my back, my head dangling over the edge of the mattress, and Alan was sitting straight up, back against the headboard of my bed, one hand resting on his soft, hairy chest. Alan, he could never leave a story unfinished.

Naomi and Wolfowitz dated steadily up until winter break. Then she went with him and his family back east for a week of skiing and board games by the fireplace. When she returned, they weren't speaking. Wolfowitz didn't take her to the Valentine's Day dance. He went stag instead and she stayed home, missing the first dance ever in her high-school career, which was a very big deal, according to Alan. A week later they were back in love, and then they were on the outs again just two weeks after that. Turns out there was talk that Mrs. Wolfowitz had walked in on something untoward between her son and Naomi while on vacation, and the Wolfowitzes no longer viewed Naomi as potential wife material.

"They were doing it?" I said.

"My aunt Esther got plastered at my parents' thirtieth anniversary party and told me that when Mrs. Wolfowitz walked in my mom was on her knees," he said.

"Oy," I said.

"Exactly," he said.

So Walter snuck in there, telling Naomi how she was a princess, a goddess, that if he were her man he would never let her go, not for a stupid fight, not for anything. And then one day in April, after a fresh rain, he walked her home from school. As they leaped over puddles and brushed their heads against the rain-soaked leaves dangling from the trees above, she let him hold her hand proudly.

"For all the world to see," I said.

"She was a prize, my mother," mused Alan. "She still is."

I rolled over and put my head on his chest, turned and faced the ceiling.

"They got married right after high-school graduation. She had me that November."

I started counting backward, November, October . . .

"Wait, I'm doing the math," I said.

"I've been doing it all my life," he said.

TWO WEEKS LATER, Alan gave me a diamond tennis bracelet. I laughed when I saw the Wolfowitz label on the inside of the box. And then I got down on my knees and pretended we were on vacation with his family.

I don't wear the bracelet much now or really at all, because where am I going to wear it. To work? On the subway? I would say I would pass it on to a daughter someday, only I'm not sure I want to have kids.

That was the problem with me and Alan. Well, that was the

first problem with me and Alan. Had we fixed it, there would have been a whole series of problems to solve after that, so we just stuck with the one. He fed me ice cream and fattened me up, then pointed out how my breasts and hips would be perfect for childbearing and nurturing. He turned parts of me into the woman he wanted, but he could never turn all of me into something I wasn't.

And then I got the job offer in New York, and decisions needed to be made.

What he said was: "You go, I'll follow."

What he did was: meet a flight attendant on one of those goddamn golf trips with his family. I saw the wedding announcement, and let's just say she's twice the shiksa I'll ever be.

For a year all I did was eat and eat and listen to him talk. And at the end, I was single again, only this time around, fat.

"WHAT HAPPENED with Wolfowitz?" I said. "Who did he end up with?"

"Who didn't he end up with?" Alan said. "Turns out my dad was right, Wolfowitz liked to play the field. He's on his third wife now. They get younger every year."

"While we just get older," I said. "It doesn't seem fair."

"You have nothing to worry about," he said, and at that moment, I couldn't figure out how to disagree. Now I have plenty to say, but then? Nothing.

DINNER IN WESTCHESTER

I agreed to go out on the first date with Gareth not because I was attracted to him, but because it had been a while. You know. A *while*. Also he asked properly, not by e-mail or instant message, but with an old-fashioned phone call. I had been spending too much time on Internet dating sites, which I often fell back on as a stopgap measure. A stopgap between *what* I can't exactly tell you, because it certainly wasn't relationships. Perhaps between winter and spring. Between my thirties and forties. Between birth and death. But to meet someone in person, names exchanged, eyes contacted, and then to receive a formal, nerve-wracking phone call made me feel like I was in high school again. Maybe we would make out, too. Maybe I would give him a hickey. Maybe I would let him get to second base.

He called me on a Tuesday evening, after dinner but before bedtime, asked about my day (long), my job (same as always, which is to say, less complicated than people think and mainly fine), and what I thought about the latest political scandal (I am never surprised). Then he popped the question: Would I join him for dinner on Friday? It could be an early meal if I had other plans, he didn't mind. He just wanted the opportunity to spend a little time with me, just an hour or two, a fraction of my day to bestow upon his unworthy self.

This charmed me, I must admit.

Instead of dinner we met for drinks postwork at an Irish pub near his place on the East Side, as I did indeed have other plans—tickets to dinner theater with my sister, Maggie, and her husband, Robert. They'd purchased them months in advance, so I couldn't say no. They liked to come to the city on a weekend at least once a month. "Because I'm down," said Robert.

"Down where?" I said.

"You know what he means," said Maggie.

The play was a historical parody—the ads for it had the word "historical" crossed out in yellow and the word "hysterical" scrawled over it in block letters—about the Last Supper. Whenever Judas tried to kiss Jesus, the audience was ordered to "drink from thine chalice." Delightful. Robert found the play "freaking hilarious" and thought it would be a good idea to recommend it to his boss. Better yet, he would get him tickets as a birthday present. Maggie agreed with him. She was a big supporter of any sort of gift-giving or, at the very least, shopping. I kept my head down in the program, contributing an occasional tidbit of information from the cast biographies.

"Did you see that Mary Magdalene was on *Law and Order*? I thought I recognized her."

"No way," said Robert.

"Way," I said.

"Honey, did you hear that?" said Robert. "*Law and Order.* I wonder if she was a criminal."

Sometimes I roll my eyes in such a fierce way that they actually hurt. I should really stop doing that.

"Maybe she was a corpse," I said.

WHEN GARETH ARRIVED, I was nursing a chardonnay at the bar and staring at the smoke-stained wood paneling behind the bartender's head. I noticed first his cowlick, combed and pressed. I parsed the syllables, envisioned the sweaty tongue of a cow feeding on a trough of water. I opened up my vision to take in the rest: Gareth was wearing a three-piece suit. I had assumed this was a low-pressure date. He had just jacked it through the roof. I suppose I did appreciate the effort, though it made me regret not going home after work to change first, as the inequality of our intentions were now rendered so painfully obvious, which is to say he had some and I did not.

Though to be fair—to me? to him?—lately I've been lazy about my appearance, slipping on clothes that require the least work, shirts without buttons, pants that I can wash and dry and wear. When I picture myself with an iron going at my clothes, it's on an old-fashioned board, and I am suddenly wearing a frilly gingham apron, perhaps with a cross-stitched homily on the front of it, and my feet are clad in simultaneously high yet sensible heels and my hair is in pin curls. Somehow I am naked under all of this, ironing, humming, steam rising from what are soon to be perfectly pressed pants. And then I reach for an old college sweatshirt and a pair of Levi's, which is what I ended up wearing when I saw Gareth.

"Don't you look fresh in that suit," I said. Gareth is an enormous man, well over six feet and probably pushing 250. The weight is in a solid block, though it's not muscle. The suit did him a favor, though. It made him look impressive rather than merely overweight. I pictured him as a king, raising a jeweled goblet to the sky, toasting some bloodthirsty victory or a peace accord between nations.

He thanked me, and sat down slowly next to me. "I like to dress up for a first date," he said. "It's just me. I'm old-fashioned." And then he quickly added, "But you, Holly, you look lovely as is. You would look perfect whether in a formal gown or, oh I don't know, hiking gear. Your beauty is transcendent."

I considered this. I didn't see myself as a transcendent beauty, though I did think my looks were from another time, all my curly hair, the curves of my hips and belly. I've recognized myself in ancient paintings in museums, but never on the pages of a fashion magazine.

"Trust me, it takes a lot of work to look like I'm not trying," I said.

I spent the next hour listening to Gareth tell me how spectacular he found me. How when he interviewed me two weeks ago he was instantly smitten, how he knew I was special right away.

"In this city it is easy to find candor in a woman," he said. "But it is usually mean-spirited. Not so with you." He looked concerned for a moment, but then his face changed to a delighted disbelief, as if he had found a hundred-dollar bill on the ground. "It's just refreshing, that's all."

Clearly he had mistaken me for someone else.

Gareth was a writer (children's books, mainly, though I did notice he'd also authored a book of satire when I searched him on Amazon) and occasional commentator for the local NPR station, and had contacted me as a source for a piece on women in modern science. (I'm a scientist. I won't go into the details of my work except to tell you that if you're a male between the ages of eighteen and thirty and you've ever peed in a cup, well, let's just say I'm *involved*.) He e-mailed me daily after the interview, ostensibly for follow-up questions, but soon enough he was sending me links of interest, followed by queries about my life, until finally he asked me out.

And now here he was, continuing his quest, a seemingly unstoppable force in the game of Getting to Know You, hurling questions about my childhood (no pets, one divorce), reading interests (Science fiction, mainly. Yes, I know, why *am* I single?), and taste in music (A former indie rocker, now retired. I still get that ringing in my ears every so often, which triggers memories of cool Budweiser drafts in plastic cups and irresistible curly haired men who wear faded T-shirts that always have back stories and who never call when they say they will, and I almost miss it. Then my chest heaves with the poison of a hundred imaginary cigarettes smoked in quick succession over the course of the night, and I smell something sour and urine-soaked, mixed with bleach, and I remember squatting above toilet seats; and then I don't miss it at all).

At the end of the hour, I apologized for having to leave, but Jesus and my choice of Veal or Chicken Marsala awaited me. I apologized also for not learning anything about him. He had focused the entire conversation on me. Sly. He asked me out again, and I agreed. He rose when I did and, pint in hand (I noticed he had two and was well into his third in an hour, but he didn't act any different, probably because of his size), escorted me to the door.

"M'lady," he said, and bowed slightly, then laughed.

I laughed, too. He made me nervous. "Sir," I responded.

If I hadn't, he would have been miserable.

IN BETWEEN the first and the second date I thought about Gareth a lot, even though I didn't know very much about him at all. I bought two of his Camilla books at lunch one day and read them in the small park in front of the lab. There was a seal from a national children's advocacy group on the cover of each colorful, oversized volume, declaring it an award-winning series, ideal for ages five to seven.

The books depicted the adventures of Camilla, a spunky young giraffe who had a longer neck than anyone else in her family. This got her into trouble sometimes: while she could see what the birds were doing in the highest trees, she often missed what was going on right below her nose. The first book involved Camilla feeling ostracized because of her height, while the second book was a morality tale about sticking your nose—or your neck, in this case—where it didn't belong.

While none of it was groundbreaking material (And how could it be? There are no new lessons left to teach children), I found endearing the heartwarming exchange between Camilla and her love interest, Otto, the roly-poly zebra who has had a crush on her since the day they met. ("No matter that you are taller than I, we both will always see the same blue skies," he declares at the end of the first book.)

I closed the book, then laid it next to me on the bench, running my hands along the smooth cover. I imagined Gareth and Maggie and Robert and me all out to dinner somewhere. He would laugh at all my jokes, especially the ones at Robert's expense, the ones Robert never gets and Maggie chooses to ignore. I wondered if he would put his arm around me when I shivered.

That was as far as I got. That was as far as I could ever get.

THE NEXT TIME we met it was a Wednesday, and we had dinner downtown near his apartment. "They know me there," he said. "I'm a regular." Regular what?

It was an Italian place, wedged in between a tiny whiskey bar and an upscale Korean restaurant. The walls were made of brick, the floor laid with shiny wood embedded with scratches, and the ceiling shone with thin strands of Christmas lights, which raced all the way from the front of the restaurant to the back. Each table also had tea lights, but beyond that, there was no lighting. Most tables were only for two, and the tables were small. You would have to sit close to someone is what I'm trying to say here. There would be nowhere else to go.

Gareth was wearing just a suit jacket and pants this time, but I could tell they had been tailor-made. I had mustered up a black sweater (the better to hide stains) and a long, loose cotton skirt, the edges of which were crumpled like a failed love letter in the trash. Gareth touched me hesitantly on the shoulder, then told me I looked beautiful.

"Black is your color," he said.

"Black is everyone's color," I said.

The host—a short, dark man with cigarette-stained teeth—greeted Gareth by name, then escorted us through the restaurant to a small patio lined with ivy. Several torches filled with citronella candles blazed as posts to the patio. There were only two other tables. Ours was clearly the best. It made me feel proud, and then my stomach lurched, as if I had stopped short in a speeding car, just moments away from an accident, but somehow, through the grace of God, had saved myself.

After Gareth ordered what I presumed was an expensive bottle of wine (the flourish of his hand, the way his voice ended on a high note, the generous nod of the waiter in response all made me feel like something important was happening), I turned to him and said, "So, Gareth, tell me about you. I don't know much except what I've read on the Internet."

"First tell me what you're going to have," he said urgently.

"I'm going to have the . . ." I glanced at the menu. "The veal, I think."

"Oh, no," he said. He inhaled, stretched his lips in pain, and shook his head. "You really don't want the veal."

"No?"

"Anything but the veal."

"Well, what do you recommend?"

"Really, anything else."

"Shrimp scamp—" I looked at him. He shook his head slowly. I closed the menu and placed it on the table. "What are you having?"

"I was thinking about having steak. We could get it for two? Any way you like, though medium rare is how I like it."

"That sounds lovely. Whatever you say. I'm easy." And then I laughed. I raised my eyebrows at him. I don't know why I did that. I didn't want to flirt with him, that much I knew.

He looked down, flushed. "Oh, I'm sure you're not easy. I'm sure you're quite the lady."

"I am, I am. I'm sorry I even said that. Anyway, tell me about you." I smiled my sweetest, most gentle smile, the one I give to small children, the elderly, and uneasy suitors. "You write children's books. That must be so rewarding."

"Oh, yes, I love children. I want to have at least three of them. Do you want to have children?"

"I'm undecided." This was true, though I knew it would discourage him. On the one hand, I would love to have children. On the other hand, then I would *have* children. That part I wasn't so sure about.

"You look like you'd be a great mother. You've got the perfect figure for childbirth, too."

I was certain this was a compliment, though it didn't feel like one.

"God, I'm such an ass," he said. "I didn't say that right at all." He flushed, then coughed. Slapped a hand to his face, then ducked down.

I wanted to reach out to him, pull his hand away from his face and pat it, calm him down. There's too much agitation over words in our lives. It seems ridiculous at times. I know my own words tumble out sometimes like ill-behaved children rolling down a hill after church while wearing their Sunday finery. Messy, messy words.

But then he added, "I do think you should at least consider it. Children."

This must be the comedy-writer part of him coming out, I thought. This must be a big joke. I laughed to test my theory. He looked disappointed. Oh, dear. He really wasn't kidding.

"Listen, Gare, I don't know if you should—"

His head snapped up. "My name is not Gare."

His voice got loud, as if he were trying to be heard above the din, only there wasn't any din, just he and I outside under the one star faintly blinking through the lights of the city. Or was it a plane?

"It's easy to skip that last syllable, I understand, but I hate it. My name is Gareth. It's a bit odd, sure, but it's a family name, and I like it. I'm big on tradition."

"Fine," I said. I wanted him to calm down. I hadn't anticipated any dramatic moments, and I didn't like it.

He leaned in closer. "Once, I went out with this girl and when she was trying to get me to do stuff she would call me Gare Bear, like that would win me over. And the only thing worse than 'Gare' is some sort of insinuation that I'm an animal, especially a large, scary, hairy animal."

"I understand," I said.

"Just—you know what? No nicknames at all. That's what works best for me."

"No nicknames. Gotcha." I picked up the menu again and stared hard at it. He tapped his fingers on the table. He tapped them sharply. "I've reconsidered," I said. "I don't want steak. I think I'll have the veal after all."

"No steak?" he said. He hadn't calmed down yet, but I think he could see where this was going. He was zooming in for a crash landing any minute.

"No steak. I just have a taste for veal tonight, and when I set my mind to something there's really no changing it." I sucked my bottom lip in under my top teeth, squinted my eyes, and tried to look tough.

Just then, the man with the yellow teeth walked up to our table with our bottle and began the wine service. "The steak is particularly good tonight," he murmured to Gareth.

And you know what? So was the veal.

I DIDN'T SEE him for a few months. He e-mailed me a couple of times, once with a link to a study reporting a higher incidence of breast cancer in women who don't give birth. Oh, I thought, so that's the way it's going to be? I responded with a link to an article proclaiming obesity a national epidemic, and then stopped replying to his e-mails after that. You can never know who is crueler, men or women. It depends on how strong your back is when it is pushed up against that wall.

I went back to my old ways, and put my profile up on yet another Internet dating site. Usually I would return to the fold with great relish, spending hours poring through the other ads, e-mailing clever questions to attractive, employed men between the ages of thirty-two and forty, and constantly updating my ad with new pictures and hilarious stories about myself in order to maintain a fresh and intriguing profile. This was always the best part: getting attention without putting too much effort into it. I mean, yes, I spent hours a night at my computer, but I never had to actually leave my home.

But eventually you had to meet them in person, and that was always disappointing. They always seemed exhausted, and not nearly as clever as in their e-mails. I'm sure I disappointed them, too. When they see "scientist" under occupation they think "sexy librarian" for some reason, but it's not the same thing at all. Maybe it's because I have glasses on in my picture, but I need those glasses to function. I'm not striving for a look—I'm practically blind.

Occasionally I would sleep with one, just to prove that I still could do it. There is a particular kind of rage I can conjure up in my eyes when I choose, and when I fuel it with alcohol, I don't need to say a word, they know they can have me for a night, for an hour, on their bed, in the bathroom at the back of the bar, on the couch in my living room. It's only awkward right at the very beginning, when they're a little surprised that it's really going to be this easy, and then again at the end, when we're saying good-bye. Because if I could just walk out silently when I'm done, that would be the best thing of all, but it is always important to them that they pretend they care, that their intentions seem good, that they take back control by offering some pretense of hope that we will somehow see each other again.

If I had wanted to see them again, I wouldn't have fucked them in the first place.

But mostly I tried to be the relatively nice girl my mother raised me to be (My father was too busy fucking his grad-student groupies to worry about how I turned out); I would go out on dates, I was dating. Yes, I will go out on a date with you, stranger who thinks referencing Voltaire and Yo La Tengo in a personal ad will make you attractive to women with good jobs, who own their own apartments within spitting distance of the park and regularly attend yoga classes. Here we are, on a date at a wine bar located equidistant from our apartments. Sure, I'll have another chardonnay; let's try something from California this time. No, I've never been engaged, never even close. I'm not that type. You are that type? Right. I'm sorry that didn't work out for you. It was for the best, obviously. It is always for the best. And I'll bet the medication is helping. It *is* helping, isn't it? Do you have any extra?

We were all just walking around this city with our hearts sadly swimming in our chests, like dying fish on the surface of a still pond. It's enough to make you give up entirely.

Still, when Gareth surfaced and e-mailed me, asking for a favor—would I meet him for a drink?—I said yes.

"WHY'D YOU bother going?" asks Maggie. I'm telling her the story of the third date, seated on the living room couch of her spacious suburban home, my legs folded under me, my head resting on my hand. Maggie speaks quietly—she has gotten quiet and careful the past few years—but with force. "I just don't understand why you go on any dates at all. You don't like anyone. Why don't you just admit that you're not interested in having a relationship? It's OK to be single. Just do it. Just *be* single."

We've just eaten steak for dinner, filet mignon, naturally. Maggie had spent the whole afternoon shopping for the dinner, she told me. What a hard worker. Her commitment to spending her husband's money was an inspiration to women everywhere.

I look at her hands, at her enormous wedding ring. Three icy karats on a solid gold band. We weren't raised to care about jewelry, but here she is, caring about jewelry. I've watched her clean it, her precious ring, swab it, shine it. Underneath the ring is a thin line of pale skin, with one brown freckle—like the ones on her lovely shoulders—in the center acting as a divider. It's her real skin underneath.

Robert is in the kitchen doing the dishes. My glass of wine is poised on a ceramic coaster they purchased on their honeymoon in Costa Rica. There was a blue chicken painted on it. They had twelve of these coasters, but they only ever used four at a time. The rest sat in a drawer. Eight blue Costa Rican chickens roosting in a drawer in Westchester.

She continues, "I have never seen you happy with a man."

"That's not true," I say. "I loved Alan. I was devastated when it ended."

"You loved Alan because he lived in Chicago. The farther away the better, that's what works for you. You know—just do these men who ask you out a favor: stop saying yes."

Maggie has tried to fix me up before, has sat me down in front of them, one after another, dinner after dinner in Westchester. A husband buffet. These single men of the suburbs were all in their forties and wealthy and really into their jobs, with one big hobby each, biking or sailing or their car. Men really do love their cars, I learned at those dinners, and if I could just love their cars, maybe I could love them, too, and they, in turn, could love me. If only.

They trotted out their divorce stories, too, which had become so practiced it was as if they were pitching a movie in Hollywood, the most important details refined into quick sentences designed to sound off the cuff and funny and memorable. ("She didn't think she had a drinking problem—she drank, no problem," said one, but I could see in his eyes that it hadn't been funny at all.) But they were back in the saddle, these men, they wanted you to know that, and being single was just a minor detail that they planned on changing as quickly as possible. If I liked what I saw. If I were interested. If I wanted to try.

Finally I told Maggie: I couldn't possibly take another bite.

Of course they were all Robert's friends, which might be part of the reason why I never liked any of them. My sister doesn't have any of her own friends anymore. She gave them up when she moved to Westchester with Robert. She sucked in his life, inflated herself like a balloon with his job and his friends and his family. She filled herself up with him until there was no room for anything else. Except for me. I've got a permanent residence somewhere in her, in the ankle or the elbow. Maybe I'm a joint.

GARETH AND I met again at the same Irish bar, this time on a Tuesday. I was a half hour late. I didn't really care. He wore another suit, crisp and pressed as I remembered, but the rest of him had collapsed: his posture sagged; his arms, his shoulders, his head, and his neck were all slung forward and drooped down as if beneath the floor there were a giant vacuum slowly sucking in his enormous frame, bone by bone, pound by pound. He was sitting in a booth near the back by the kitchen, underneath a framed sepia-toned picture of a baseball player at bat. The frame was crooked. He did not rise when I joined him. I tried to straighten the frame as I sat, but it dipped down on the other side so the player and his bat were askew, aiming a shot at the sky.

"Thanks for meeting me," said Gareth.

There were three empty pint glasses in front of him, and he gripped a full fourth one.

"I will make this brief. I was sad when our relationship didn't work out. I felt very close to you immediately, as I told you at the time. I thought you and I had a real future together, even though we didn't agree on the whole children issue, but I think you would have come around. So I have to wonder why it didn't work out."

I looked around me to see if anyone was listening. "We only went out on one date," I said.

"Twice," he corrected.

"I would hardly count meeting for a quick beer a date," I said.

"To me, it was a date," he said. Something in his voice, a tenderness unfamiliar in my daily existence, convinced me to play along.

"It was a date, sure," I said soothingly. I inched toward the edge of the booth.

"So after two dates and several phone calls and countless e-mails I have to wonder, why didn't it work out?"

I sat there and waited to hear a theory, and then I realized he was actually asking me a question. "Oh, you want me . . . ? OK. I just wasn't interested. It's not a big deal, you're simply not my type."

He looked down, and made an impatient noise. Then he drew himself up, pulled his shoulders back, looked at the ceiling, and then proclaimed, "It's because I'm fat."

"You're not fat," I said.

"Hey, I know I'm fat. My mother says I'm fat, my doctor says I'm fat. Don't bother lying."

I struggled. There wasn't a correct response. "I didn't come here to discuss your weight," I said.

"But you think I'm fat, right?"

I rested my head against the back of the booth, felt my back flatten against it. I shrugged my shoulders, swung my hands up in the air. "Do you want me to be the asshole here? Because I can be the asshole if that's going to make you happy. Tell me what you're looking for, because I'm more than willing to give it to you if it's going to make you feel better."

"Be my girlfriend," he pleaded.

ROBERT COMES into the room, dish towel on his shoulder, shaking droplets of water off his hand.

"So how did you leave it with him?" says Maggie.

"Let's just say . . . I was the asshole," I say.

Robert laughs, presumably at my use of a curse word. "Are you breaking hearts again?" he says. "Don't worry, the right man is out there for you, just waiting for the right moment to sweep you off your feet."

Maggie takes a sip from her wineglass and looks away. I was sorry I had made her sad. Robert notices it, too, and reaches his hand down to her shoulder, but she swats it away, as if it were a fly circling endlessly around her. And then I see her do something familiar. I have done it so many times myself I know exactly what is going on in her head at this moment. I see her pull into herself. I see her recede. But I don't think she has much room for herself in there. Me, I'm hollow inside. There is only me, just me. I know that someday she'll get sick of being full of Robert. I know she'll puke him out of her system. But she'll never get rid of me. I'm in her blood.

GARETH CONTACTED me one last time. I didn't tell Maggie that part. It somehow seemed better that she thought me only guilty of my usual callousness. He sent an e-mail a week after our last meeting. In it he apologized in a sincere and clean fashion.

He had been having trouble finishing his latest book, he explained. He had been drinking too much, pints and pints of beer every night of the week, which was unlike him. "I'm not a drinker," he wrote. "Not like that."

There was an anger and confusion inside of him, and he did not know where to direct it so he had turned it on me, he explained. Well, he had turned it on a half dozen women he had dated in the last year, but of all of the ones he had tried to contact then, I was the only one who had responded.

"It is just hard in this city sometimes. Surely you know that." (I did, of course.) "Sometimes you just need to get it out. And you were the one who agreed to see me. It wasn't fair. There have been others who were much worse to me. You were, in fact, just fine."

"I would have treated you like gold," he wrote. "I say that not to imply that you missed out on something great, but just so you know that I had only the best of intentions."

He asked for my forgiveness. He italicized the words for emphasis. If I could just give him that, he said he would feel better, he could move on toward attempting a life of clarity.

Telling him he was fat—that was not the worst thing I could have done to him. He already knew that. Never replying to that e-mail, that was when I was the asshole. But I could not find one word inside of me, neither kind nor cruel, to give to him. I had nothing left inside.

I TAKE THE Metro-North home from Westchester. I cannot get home fast enough. Commuter trains should have wings, I think. Wings on engines.

In my apartment I turn on the computer, speed-dial my dating site. I survey the profiles and reflect on the reasons why I should get to know them better, why they are the one for me, if I am the one for them.

"I am sick of neurotic New York women," says one. "I know what I want. You should also."

Another swears he's funny. He wants to make me laugh. He is all about *the laughter*.

A third has the profile name "No_Strings_Attached" and he is young and his jaw is set like a rock. "Strings are for puppets," he writes. "I am not a puppet. Are you?"

No. I am not a puppet.

ISLAND FEVER

Melanie moved to the island around the same time my marriage with Will was disintegrating into tiny pieces. I had first started noticing the pieces after an enormous fight, when he told me, "I can see now how someone could hate you." Bam! It was like confetti shot out of a toy gun. The pieces started high in the air, spiraled around our eyes and lips and hands, and finally landed at our feet, covering the carpeting of our home. We would try so hard not to step on those pieces, but whenever I walked from the bedroom to the kitchen in the morning to make coffee and get myself out the door before he woke up, I'd step on something, like that time I got drunk in front of his mother at lunch and talked too loudly for a long time and ordered two desserts and ate half of each.

"You're a spoiled child," the piece of our marriage would squawk.

Will, too, would try to tread lightly, and he was better at it than I was, but sometimes the pieces got stuck on the bottom of his shoes and would make noise, like when he was driving and put his foot down on the gas when he thought it was safe for speeding, or hit the break hard, too hard, when he thought a cop might be coming up behind him.

"You're reckless," the little piece would intone. "And you're a little dumb, to be quite honest."

Eventually we were so afraid of stepping on our marriage, we began to tiptoe around all the time. It became perfectly silent in the house, which was good, but after a while the balls of my feet began to hurt, and then slowly every part of my body followed. It freaked me out at first, but then I remembered the nerve endings to your entire body end in your feet. The tiptoes were destroying me.

Melanie's marriage fell apart for no good reason except for personalities that didn't mix when things got rough. She had married Doug straight out of college, just like I had married Will. I was maid of honor at her wedding, and she was matron of honor at mine. When things went bad Melanie and I stuck together, and all our other friends left us behind. It's like there's this stink associated with the both of us, because we were too lazy or crazy or fat to make our marriages work. We did get a little fat, the both of us, sure, but that's not why the marriages didn't work. Only Melanie and I can understand this, and everyone else could kiss our asses. So our friendship strengthened as everything else crumbled. It was all we had left in the wreckage.

THE LAST TIME I saw Melanie before her divorce was when she packed the last of her possessions into Bitsy McSherman's massive SUV. She was moving to Bitsy's house on the island, a ferry ride away from her husband, her family, and me, her best friend. I came by to say good-bye, and to offer interference between her and Doug if necessary. When I pulled up, Bitsy was in the front seat of the SUV, her outline faint behind a tinted window. Melanie was shuffling boxes and suitcases around in the trunk, reconfiguring the layout a dozen times until everything fit, so she'd never have to return for anything left behind. Doug was standing in the living room, staring out the front window.

I walked over to the window. I didn't think I could make him feel better—I'm not good at that sort of thing; celebrating the good times is more my cup of tea—I just wanted to see his face, to see what he was feeling. He was dressed like he needed to do his laundry, in a tie-dyed T-shirt with a Ben & Jerry's logo on it, and baggy jeans. His neck and back were slouched, and his hands were shoved firmly in his front pockets, as if that were the only thing keeping him standing. I noticed for the first time he was going bald.

I waved at him through the window, and he waved back. A row of shrubs separated us, so we just stood there, on opposite sides of the window, and looked at each other. Melanie went back in for one more box, and then she said something to Doug. I couldn't hear what she said, but I saw Doug's mouth move in response, and I read his lips.

"Don't bother," he said.

Melanie came back outside, and I followed her down to the car. She opened the door to the backseat, and threw her last box in there. There was a small jade plant in the box, the baby stalk of which had just begun to burst with thumb-shaped leaves. I found this surprisingly optimistic. There were also some photo albums, a high school yearbook, and a tiny table lamp, the kind you get in college for late-night reading in bed, so you don't wake up your roommate. Melanie slammed the door shut. Such vigor, I thought. She hadn't had this much energy in a while. I guess she was fueled by desperation, though I hadn't known it was that bad. Shows you what I know.

Melanie opened her arms to me, and I realized I was supposed to hug her, so I did. She made me promise to come visit, and I made her promise to come back soon.

"Don't stay on the island too long," I said. "We don't want to lose you there."

She got in the car, and I pulled my keys out of my pocket and started toward my own car. I clenched and unclenched the keys in my fist.

Melanie rolled down the windows.

"Jemma, come here."

I walked back to the car and faced her.

"This is Bitsy. Bitsy, this is Jemma. Jemma is my friend."

I waved, and so did she. I stared at her, trying to memorize everything about her, as if I might have to identify her in a lineup someday. She could have been a plain woman, with her long stern nose, the bridge of which was like a bullet, and her tight, pale purple lips, and small dark eyes like black pearls. She looked old, I thought, at least as old as Melanie's mother. But the rest of her was extraordinary in a way, maybe because she was so different from everyone I knew. Her hair was a beautiful shade of bronze, a huge and styled and shiny mane, and her ears and neck and her wrists were dripping with gold and diamonds; diamond earrings, diamonds bigger than my engagement ring, and a thick braided gold necklace with a huge diamond teardrop hanging from it, and gold bracelets, so many of them, up and down her tanned, muscular arms. The car smelled of a rich perfume. I got a little high off it.

"How delightful to meet one of my Melanie's friends. At last." Bitsy stretched her arm around the back of Melanie's seat.

"Well, any friend of Melanie's . . . ," I said. I didn't bother to finish it. I was certain Bitsy and I had nothing in common.

"Yes," said Bitsy. "And all that jazz." She revved the engine softly and rhythmically, as if she were tapping her foot on it.

"You take care of my girl," I said.

Bitsy smiled kindly, but then raised her eyebrows too high, and her face changed into something sinister, and I thought for a second that she was going to kidnap Melanie forever, and that I would never get her back.

IN COLLEGE, I had clung to Melanie, night after night. We used to get together and drink until we saw double, and laugh so hard we could barely stand. Then we would walk home, arm in arm, from a party or from one of the bars in the U District, weaving up and down the empty, rainy streets, across campus, wherever we felt like walking, because we were young and drunk and it felt good to use our limbs. Me and Melanie, and then Will and Doug, too.

There were other friends, other girls, but no one stuck like me. For a brief while Melanie had a fascination with this girl with a stutter, Sarah Lee, visiting from some East Coast city, Philadelphia or Boston. Some sort of town of urban blight. They worked together at this bakery near the expressway entrance. In the mornings commuters would come in for coffee and a muffin, and in the afternoon they'd get the stoner crowd, hungry for chocolate-chip cookies, or their pies, which they were known for, cherry and apple, fresh from the oven. I ate more than a few slices when I was in college. I know how sweet they tasted.

I never fully understood Melanie's interest in her. Yes, Sarah Lee was a pleasant girl, pretty enough, and when she laughed it was loud, and excited, with huge gasps of air at the end, and it made everyone—not me, of course—want to laugh, too. And I remember in particular we all enjoyed looking at her outfits— she was always tearing apart clothes she got at the Value Village and restructuring them into something cool and different and new. But she had these unfortunate, large ears, and of course, that stutter, and who was she anyway? Just another girl you work with at a part-time job. A little bit younger, a little too enthusiastic. Innocent, perhaps. At first anyway. A transplant trying to find herself, when Melanie and I already knew exactly who we were.

But Melanie always took to eccentrics, so when I wasn't around, there was Sarah, which was fine. I understand. It's good to have a partner, a wingman of sorts. And then after a while Sarah was around even when I was there, and I didn't like that one bit. I never got to know her that well because I never tried. I only knew that she was always there, as if she were a new next-door neighbor who keeps borrowing sugar, and then eggs, and then milk. Eventually you let her know you can't spare anything else. Even if your cupboard is completely full. Because eventually enough is enough.

MELANIE'S REPORTS from the island made her sound happy, and I liked to hear it. Contentment, I wondered what that felt like. Bitsy had offered her a residency program of sorts, she explained. Melanie had studied landscape design in college, and Bitsy had offered up part of her land as a canvas. Plus Bitsy was introducing her around to all the rich folks on the island, and Melanie was starting to get some work on other estates.

"They're awful competitive out here," she told me. "You plant one row of tulips in someone's front yard on a Monday, and by Tuesday you've got phone calls to do the same at four other homes. Only—twice, and bigger."

"The mysterious case of the multiplying tulips," I said.

Mostly Melanie talked about Bitsy, her benefactor. They had met outside the Asian Art Museum—Bitsy had noticed her sketching the sunset through Volunteer Park—and Melanie was obviously fascinated with her. It was always: Bitsy bought a new couch, Bitsy is decorating a diplomat's house, Bitsy knows *every-one* on the island.

She owned a lot of land, and had used her home there as a weekend getaway for years. Up and down the West Coast she was a famous interior designer, that's what Melanie told me. But Bitsy said she liked how she was just island folk whenever she was there on the weekend. She liked walking around what passed for a downtown in her Wellies, and waving hello across the aisle in the grocery store, and reading the Sunday *Seattle Times* at the café near the ferry landing.

"They call her 'Ditsy Bitsy' around the island," Melanie said. Her voice didn't change when she talked about Bitsy, so I could never tell how she actually felt about her. She was like a newscaster reporting the facts, not allowed to express an opinion. News about Bitsy at eleven. I guess she was afraid to feel anything. Bitsy had given her a home, after all.

I wanted to believe she had a smile on her face, though.

So I would get the weekly report from Melanie on Sunday mornings. She would call from the main house while Bitsy was at church. ("She's not religious," Melanie explained. "She's just community-oriented.") That's when I would get the full break-down of Bitsy-related activity, mostly revolving around her social life. Some of the time Melanie would talk about her work on the island, and that's when her voice would be at its most animated.

"They're doing such cool things here, Jemma." And she'd go on and on about solar power and public gardens and even the compost pile. Twenty minutes she'd spend talking about a compost pile, like she had never seen one before, like she hadn't grown up with one in her backyard, like she hadn't written a dozen papers on them in college, like she hadn't volunteered at the composting center all of her senior year. But I suppose the air is a little fresher out on the island, away from the big buildings and all the cars. Melanie always wanted more from her environment.

She never talked about Doug, and I didn't bring him up. Between the two of us there was a silent agreement to talk only about things that moved us forward. We never could find any sense in holding on to the past. Melanie had jumped ship after just four years of marriage.

"When it isn't going to work, you just know it. And I'm not in the mood to get my hands dirty fixing it." That's what she told me when she called me the first time from Bitsy's place, and I let it go after that. I was sure her family and his family were giving her enough grief. I didn't want to add to the mix, and anyway I had my own problems. It made no sense to take her down with me.

WHENEVER SARAH LEE stuttered, I talked over her. At first I was just finishing her sentences, and I don't think I fully realized what I was doing. But then her increased presence in our lives re-quired direct action. I started replying before she was finished with her sentence, not even knowing what the question was, or even if she was asking a question in the first place. Sometimes I would change the subject, or I would laugh even if it wasn't funny. I just didn't want anyone to hear what she had to say.

I knew what I was doing. I knew what I was saying, how I was making her feel. I knew I was being cruel. I just didn't care. She'd survive without Melanie, she'd move on to someone new. She'd find twenty new best friends in the next year. I was the one who had nowhere else to go. I had already found my home.

AFTER A FEW months at Bitsy's, right around when spring started to kick in and the land all around us turned to bloom and the sun started burning off the clouds early in the day, killing the fresh rain of the mornings, Melanie called me for our Sunday-morning chat with the latest news. I had really started to look forward to her calls, especially since Will and I had mostly checked out on each other. He had moved some stuff out—I guess to his folks' place—but hadn't bothered to tell me. Half of his closet was empty, a dozen dress shirts gone one morning, and he thought I wouldn't notice? Or maybe he just didn't care.

"Bitsy's at war!" Melanie said before I'd even finished "Hello."

"Ooh, with who?" I put my feet up on the kitchen table, leaned my head against the wall. I could see the neighbor's dog sniffing in our backyard.

"With Madame Vanessa."

"No! Why can't she just leave that little old lady alone?" I said.

Madame Vanessa lived next door to Bitsy and Melanie. She was old and French and rich. Her son had bought her the house for retirement and as a weekend spot for their family a decade ago, where she had lived peacefully until Bitsy moved in next door. Suddenly there were problems with the property lines (Bitsy claimed—and won—an extra half acre), and most recently Bitsy disapproved of their disparate landscape designs at the front of their plots (a problem solved by Madame Vanessa's subsequent hiring of Melanie who duplicated the look of Bitsy's land).

And now, apparently, it was Madame Vanessa's fence. It was chain link while Bitsy's was white picket, and Bitsy couldn't stand it.

"She's done everything under the sun to change this woman's mind. First she sent her clippings from a catalogue of a fence she preferred. Then she invited her over for tea so she could look out the window and see how awful the fences look next to each other. But of course this woman is perfectly happy with her fence!"

"Of course. Chain link is lovely," I laughed.

"She has dogs, and they're massive. She says they would just scratch up a nicer fence. Anyway, Bitsy just sits around coming up with plots to get her way. I think she's losing her mind."

"Are you all right there?"

"Yes, of course. I just work all the time, and Bitsy's here only on the weekends. But still . . ."

"Lonely?"

"Yes. Will you come visit?"

I agreed to visit in a few weeks. I wanted the chance to suck in a bit of the energy Melanie seemed to be bursting with. I'll admit I was afraid that, when I returned, Will would have moved out completely. But if he was going to go, he should just do it already. I just didn't want to be the one responsible for kicking him out the door.

SARAH LEE CALLED me on it eventually. In a bathroom, in a bar, hands washed, bottles resting on the counter.

"You don't like me," she said. She wore a tight yellow T-shirt with a tractor on it. She had drawn swirling birds all around the tractor.

"Like" was said with a stutter.

I picked up my bottle and sipped it. I stared at her like I hated her. "I like you just fine," I said.

"No you don't," she said. She was drunk. She could never say no to another, I had noticed, and someone was *always* offering to buy her one.

"You're right. I don't."

"I don't like you, either," she said, but I knew she was lying.

ON THE FERRY RIDE OVER, I sat in the truck, hands gripping and releasing the steering wheel. Most people get out and enjoy the view of the sound, the mountains to the west, and the tips of the other islands, or they wave good-bye to the city behind them. Not me, I just looked at the other cars. I was surrounded by them—two lines to the right, a line to the left, and cars in front and back, stretching the length of the boat. I simply sat there and waited in this frozen line. It was a pretty day, too, and the skies were clear. I held the steering wheel. Grip. Release. I hadn't known how badly I had wanted to leave my house for the weekend until I had done just that.

Ask me why I took the truck and not the Cavalier. Go ahead, ask me. I took the truck and left Will with the Cavalier so that it wouldn't be as easy to move his stuff. I had left before him in the morning, and I hadn't even told him I was going the night before. I stuck a note in the oversized glass ashtray near the front door, where we stored our keys and spare change. Let him see what it feels like to be the last to know.

One of the ferry workers knocked on my window, and I pulled my head back in surprise and hit the seat.

"You all right, ma'am?"

My husband is leaving me, I wanted to say. He used to spend all his time trying to make me laugh, and I used to think he was funny. Now we can't even smile at each other in the morning. I'm twenty-seven and I've already failed. I'm going to be alone. I'm going to have to date strangers. Someone is going to try to kiss me awkwardly after he buys me Chinese food and takes me to a Sandra Bullock romantic comedy. I'm going to have to start carrying gum in my purse. And lipstick. And I'm going to have to lose weight. Goddammit.

Instead I say: "Yes, why do you ask?"

"Well, you keep honking your horn."

I looked down at my hands. I thought they were high up on the wheel at twelve o'clock, in anticipation of driving. Turns out they were dead center, in anticipation of disaster.

ON THE ISLAND, Melanie and I were drinking each other under the table and I didn't care. I couldn't believe how thirsty I was for the taste of beer. It was like we were back in college, when drinking was a sport. Then there were a million bars to go to, but out on the island, as Melanie told me, there are only three.

"The people who live in the trailers go to the pub on the other side of the island, and the place across the street"—she motioned with her eyes—"is for the family types."

"So who's left?" I said.

"I don't know. The in-betweens, I guess."

We played pool and pinball for a while, and then I saw the jukebox in the corner of the room. I emptied the contents of my change purse into my hand, and then I dug around the bottom of my purse for more quarters. I was going to play every single song I knew the words to tonight, and I was going to sing along at the top of my lungs. When I looked at the jukebox I was not disappointed. It was as if they had transported the radio in the truck my mother had when I was a child, and programmed it into this jukebox. She used to drive me to school and play all the songs on the rock station at full blast, and we would both sing along.

Man, Mick Jagger. I used to love Mick Jagger. Why'd he have to go and get old? Or was he always old? Oh, the Eagles. The *Eagles*. The Who, wow, are you kidding me? "Eminence Front," that was one of the first videos I ever saw. *Won't you come and join the party, dress to kill.* And I have to play some Beatles songs. The Beatles will never die. I should really go to bars more. Why did I stop going to bars? Or maybe I could get a jukebox for the apartment? Will likes music. Will would like a jukebox. Will, Will, Will.

I saw that Melanie was talking to two guys at the bar. As I walked across the room, I tried to add a little strut to my walk, a saunter, a little shake of the ass. *Shake your ass.* I liked that song, too. Where had I heard that song? That Hugh Grant movie. The one with the weird kid and the mom who tried to kill herself.

I was never going to have children, was I? And we had talked about it. It had been *discussed*. There was a time when Will and I thought we needed to make something more out of the two of us besides excellent dinner companions, a great couple to have over for potluck. He works in software, she's a media buyer. He understands that college football is much more interesting than pro, and she's sincerely interested in your exercise regimen, even though she wouldn't step foot in a gym. He still has a good weed connection, and she likes to drink chardonnay as much as you do, honey.

One of the guys talking to Melanie was cute, lean and tan, though he needed a haircut. He smiled at me as I sat on my stool. He had the whitest teeth, like he'd eaten an apple every day of his life. It was too much for me to handle, the gleam of his smile.

His friend was short, and puffy with alcohol, you could tell, with his red nose, ruddy cheeks almost like he'd been running and needed to catch his breath. He was smiling like a clown, lips clamped together, cheeks raised high.

"This is Brock and Ryan. They run the nursery on the island," said Melanie. Ryan, the man with the perfect smile, shook my hand. Brock opened his mouth, but only garbled words came out. I thought he might be retarded, but I couldn't be sure.

Suddenly Brock spun around in a circle, and then started a little dance to the tale of the brown-eyed girl; hands clenched in fists, shoulders and arms grooving, the slightest wag of his behind, and sway of his legs. He bobbed his head in my direction, then pointed toward an open space at the back of the bar.

Ryan leaned in to me and said, "He wants to dance with you."

"Go on, dance with him," said Melanie. "He's fine. I know him. He's just really drunk."

I looked back and mouthed, "I'm going to kill you," to Melanie. She laughed, and so did Ryan. Wait—was that his hand on her hip? Not that I cared, only I wanted her to tell me if something was going on between them. I was her best friend. She could tell me the truth. In fact, she should tell me the truth. Here I was, here on this island, waiting for it.

Brock took my hand, raised his arm, and spun me awkwardly underneath it. I let out a laugh, and he started to pull me toward the dance floor. I really was going to kill her.

But then as soon as we started dancing, I was glad I hadn't fought him. Every limb was electrified. I was dancing backup on *Solid Gold*, I was breaking all the records on *Dance Fever*, I was shaking my caboose on *Soul Train*. I moved my hips and my chest and arms and then neck and head. I jumped, I glided. Sweat formed at my temples, and brushed my breasts and shoulders. *I can't get no. Satisfaction. Hey hey hey.* I shook it like the world was on fire and only the force of my body could put out the flames.

What my partner was doing, I'll never know. That dance was about me. The dance is always about me.

At the end of the song he said slowly, words struggling out of his mouth, "You dance good."

I hugged him, and in the sweaty embrace, I could feel the hard throb of his groin against me. I pushed him back with one hand, not that hard, even, and he stumbled, then fell to the ground. It's always the same, I thought. The same tricks. Brock stayed on the floor.

I could kick him right now, I thought, letting the image hang in my head for moment, a small present to myself. Kicking and kicking in the gut and groin, kicking all the life out of him so I could have it for my own. He opened his mouth, and he made a noise. It reminded me of an animal braying. No one would say a thing if I kicked him. No one would blame me.

Instead I turned and walked back to Melanie and Ryan.

"Your friend is way too drunk to be out right now," I said. I looked right into Ryan's eyes, telegraphed that he needed to take care of his business. He flashed his brilliant teeth, and the bar glowed from it. Melanie stifled a laugh, and I turned and looked back at Brock, who had now lain down on the floor, arms at his side like a corpse.

"Shit," said Ryan, and he was gone to the dance floor. He bent down on his hands and knees, whispering sweet nothings in Brock's ear, hoping to make his friend rise from his deep, drunken sleep.

"There's no helping that guy," I said.

"Ryan'll take care of him," said Melanie, bored. "And he'll be fine tomorrow. He does this all the time. He's always fine in the morning."

Ryan pulled him up by his arms, chest, and then his legs, and leaned his friend against him. They stumbled through the bar, toward the front door.

I looked at my beautiful friend and I thought of the hopeful jade plant.

"How long are you going to stay out here?" I said. "On this island. Seriously."

"As long as it takes," she said.

_____

AFTER A WHILE, Sarah Lee didn't come around anymore, and then after that she drifted off to art school somewhere in Oregon.

"Good riddance," I said.

"Why?" said Melanie. "I liked her."

"Yeah, and I think she *really* liked you," I said.

"What does that mean?" said Melanie. "What does that *mean*?" She pushed my arm playfully.

"You know what that means," I said, and I raised my eyebrows. "I don't like the way she looked at you."

And we laughed and laughed. At Sarah Lee's expense. Because while I told Melanie I didn't like the way Sarah Lee looked at her, what I really didn't like was the way Melanie looked at Sarah Lee.

AT LAST CALL Melanie and I had eyes like stewed tomatoes. We decided to walk home.

"It's only a half mile up the road," she said. "And we're on an island. We're safe as kittens."

"No way," I said. I was a grown-up city girl now. I didn't walk home drunk anymore.

"Yes, yes, yes. We'll drive my car back in the morning and get your bag." She put her arm around my shoulder and squeezed me off the bar stool. "Come on. It's going to be OK."

We stumbled off into the night, walking in the center of the moonlit road. Away from the city lights, I could see a million stars spotting the sky, little bits of light holding back the dark. I could see the outlines of the trees in silhouette, and I could smell the dampness of the greenery. Melanie made me inhale deeply.

"Isn't it fantastic out here? Isn't this what it's all about?"

We dragged our feet at times, and ran, laughing, in short spurts. I almost fell in a ditch. I noticed Melanie had lost some weight, and I silently cursed her. My nose was running and I rubbed it. Melanie did a cartwheel in the center of the road.

"We're almost there!" she yelled. "Let's cut across—" She motioned to the lawn, then hopped the white picket fence bordering the land and began to march diagonally, away from the road. "Oh, no, wait, wait. First you *have* to see this." She ran back to the road and dragged me by my hand, until we were standing in front of two houses. "You have to stand back for the full effect." We walked backward until we were standing on the far side of the road, away from the houses, underneath a small streetlight.

"Do you see?" She gestured toward the houses.

"What am I looking at?"

"The fences. Do you see the difference?"

I looked at Bitsy's impeccable white picket fence, and then I looked at Madame Vanessa's simple chain-link fence. A black Lab sniffed near the front gate, and gave one short bark. I leaned against the streetlight, and then lowered myself to the ground. I needed a minute to pass judgment.

"It kills her. It just *kills* her," said Melanie.

"It's not that bad," I said, and it wasn't. All across America people had different fences from their neighbors'. Why did Bitsy get to be different?

"I mean I sort of get why she feels this way," Melanie said. She sat down next to me, pulled her legs into a cross-legged position. "This is her sanctuary, this home. It's her way of getting away from the world. I think she feels like the other fence is invading her space."

"But it's not her decision to make," I said. "It's this woman's property. She can do whatever she likes with it as long as it's not hurting anyone. And I'm sorry, aesthetics do not count."

"I'm not saying she's right, Jemma," said Melanie sharply. "I'm just saying I see her point."

I pulled my legs up, till my knees almost hit my chin. I looked up at the bugs milling about the streetlight.

She pointed. "See how that other fence is so much taller. It sticks out like a sore thumb."

"Yeah, I see it. I just don't get why it's such a big deal."

We were quiet for a minute. The dog barked again. I heard a car engine running, and the sound of tires on gravel, and a minute later, a car was in front of us, passing us, and heading up the hill. They honked.

"Bitsy says . . ."

"Bitsy says what?" I snapped.

"She says she loves me," said Melanie quietly. "She wants to take care of me."

"*Loves you* loves you? Or just loves you?"

"Both. Well, the first one. I don't know."

"Do you love her?"

"She says she loved me right away, the minute she saw me she had to have me, that's what she says. That I energize her. Bring her to life."

I traced the shape of a heart with my finger in the dirt.

"I don't know what else to do right now but to let someone love me. It's better than not being loved at all, don't you think?"

I didn't know what to say to my friend. I knew that I was supposed to open my mouth and wisdom, preferably of the sage variety, should effortlessly tumble out. That's not my strong suit, though. I know that there are a handful of things to be admired about me. I am pleasant to look at, even with twenty extra pounds on me. I can be funny and I can be direct in an inoffensive way and people seem to trust me right away, think I look like a nice girl. I have an even tone to my voice. I am a natural blond.

But I am the first to admit I have many more limitations. I am selfish, I am that spoiled child that my husband likes to call me. I am smart but not smart enough to have foresight. When I took the truck and left the sedan, it was a major act of triumph for me, and one that was inspired mainly by a television commercial for 4X4s. I had to really think about it. I don't like to think that hard too often. You would think I could help a friend, that my back would be strong because I am young and healthy. But my back is actually weak, because I have never had to use it before, not once. I have never lifted a heavy object, and I certainly have never had to carry someone who needed my help.

I could have fought for her. I could have told her that she was loved, not just by me, but by many other people. That she shouldn't fear being alone. That I was her friend, and I would take care of her. But in reality she didn't have too many friends in the first place, and she'd have even fewer left as soon as they found out she was shacked up with some middle-aged lady on this hippie island. And I wasn't doing much better at taking care of myself; how much could I offer to her?

Instead I said, "Did you lose weight? You really do look great."

AFTER A FEW DAYS of clean air—I returned home the morning of Bitsy's return because Melanie thought it would be easier that way, and I suppose she was right; I wouldn't have to report back a thing because if I didn't see her, she didn't exist—I headed back to the city, to my apartment, to my life. While Melanie had clean air all around her, the air in my home was now polluted. When I left, the house had been quiet and (I thought) clean. When I returned, I discovered the remains of my marriage had turned. Our marriage was now sour milk, moldy bread, and unpaid bills, stacked high in a corner. And I was the only one left to clean it up, because Will was gone, for good as it turned out.

With him he took: the contents of the bottom three drawers of our bedroom chest, and the rest of his side of the closet; all of his shoes from the front closet, his favorite umbrella, and his rain gear; the fancy espresso machine and the French press that we got as a wedding present from his boss, plus some silverware we got from his rich aunt from San Francisco; books, tons of them, all of them, really, because I'm not much for reading; the gray suede couch he used for his Sunday naps, and the television set, the combination DVD/VCR player, the CD player, the speakers, and the entertainment center that had housed all of them. We had bought all of those last items new in the last year. I was bummed they were gone.

What he left behind was: my clothes; the rest of the kitchen appliances and flatware, including the coffee machine, for which I was grateful because I always favored drip coffee; as well as the kitchen table and chairs, the bedroom chest, the beautiful wooden bed frame and all the bedding (except, strangely, for one pillow); the big red leather chair I bought with my Christmas bonus two years ago; all of our photo albums, which sat on the otherwise empty bookshelves; and the table near the front door, the oversized glass ashtray that sits upon it, and all of the change contained within it.

I looked for a note in the ashtray and also on the refrigerator, which he used for note-leaving sometimes. There was none.

I sat on the couch and stared at the space where the entertainment center used to be. I realized I would be driving the truck from now on because of the decision I had made a few days previous, and now I had to live with it. The wrong car, I thought to myself. I picked the wrong car. I'm stuck now. I'm stuck. I made the wrong decision. I am completely stuck.

HE KNOWS A LOT of old jokes, she's heard them all before. She wants to hear new jokes. He wants her to cook more, look at all of these appliances; she wants him to try just a little harder to make her laugh. If you could just try a little harder. Just try to be interesting. Do something.

MEAN BONE

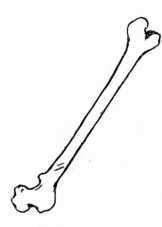

I cut a man once, she tells her husband. She says this after they've been married for two years, and he's certain he already knows everything about her. This is just her way of letting him know: Boy, were you wrong.

I cut him right here. She slid her finger sharply across his upper thigh, near the groin. I slashed him. She is sitting straight up, neck and head held high, no pretense, no guise, just her.

Maggie, come on. You did no such thing. His wife is the nicest woman he knows.

I did, too, Robert.

And when did this alleged felony occur?

Robert has been watching too much *Law & Order,* she thinks.

The summer before my junior year of college, she says. I went a little crazy.

THAT SUMMER, her father made her live with him in Evanston, in a huge, dusty rented house with wood floors and walls so dark and cool, she felt like she was living in an icebox.

He was running a writing program as he did every summer, at a school there. He was a famous writer who led a fancy, famous life that she and her older sister, Holly, were usually absent from because he had abandoned them when they were young and moved to California.

But once a year he would be somewhere wonderful, usually on the West Coast, and they would join him, and it was always exciting because there was an ocean! And blue skies! And there was silence, too, and wide expanses of land and trees and sand that were so enormous and inspirational that Maggie and Holly would forget for exactly three months that they were supposed to hate their father. They would nestle together under the stars at night, in his backyard, and talk about their favorite constellations, while their father was off screwing one of his students.

Evanston was not California. Evanston had a lot of trees, but the houses were too close together, and flaccid Lake Michigan was a poor substitute for the untamed, wild beauty of the Pacific Ocean. Evanston made Maggie want to nap all day long.

It was the last summer she was supposed to live with him— her sister, Holly, had already made it out of the system with a self-financed trip to Europe; she sent weekly postcards from beautiful cities, each one reporting both a major work of art she had seen and how many beers she had drunk the night before— and every day, every meal, every conversation with her father made Maggie feel like she had some sort of terminal illness, that she was slowly being killed by a potent and painful boredom.

But as she kept most of her feelings inside—mostly because it was more fun in there, but also because she was never proven wrong that way—that boredom turned liquid, like pus inflating a sore.

AND THEN HE made me get a job, she says now to Robert. He wanted me to be an assistant at the English Department. Staple papers. Make copies. File. Or he said he could get me a job doing research for a friend of his doing a book on feminist iconography in contemporary music.

Robert raises his eyebrows.

Madonna, she says.

That actually sounds fun, honey, he says. You didn't want to do that?

I didn't want to do anything he wanted me to do, she says. Exasperated, like: you should know how I feel about him by now. She feels like stinging today.

SHE GOT A JOB waiting tables at a country club within walking distance of their house. She had to wear a black polyester dress with a white collar as a uniform. There were tiny black buttons down the front that buttoned nothing, they just hung off the dress. She was told to wear her hair back, so she fastened her thick auburn hair with silver Goody barrettes she bought at the

7-Eleven. She bought black flats with comfortable soles and a dozen packs of tan nylons at Payless. And then she went next door, to the makeup outlet shop, and bought a tube of frosted pink lipstick.

When she walked downstairs the first morning for work, her father said, "Jesus Christ, I didn't send you to Princeton so you could look like the fucking maid."

HE HAD A POINT, says Robert.

Maggie stares at him. Lately, each time he opens his mouth he makes her love him less and less. She is trying to decide if he is doing this on purpose or if she is just now realizing for the first time how much he sucks.

Nothing wrong with a little hard work, she says. You can't argue with that.

SHE TOOK THE lunch shifts that summer, waiting on the wives and children of the members who were too lazy to cook their own grilled cheese sandwiches at home. The wives, some older, some younger, were sharp-tongued and particular, and most days operated with a fierce sense of entitlement. Maggie was someone to do their bidding (Never fast enough, never perfectly, they would sigh, as she brought them their food), and consistently neglected to thank her. Their children were better mannered and more respectful—they at least occasionally thanked her for her service—but Maggie still found them wasteful; they ordered food just to take one bite, they heaped out gobs of ketchup they would never use, and they often ordered sugary drink after sugary drink, until Maggie was certain their teeth would turn brown before her eyes. She was silent throughout all of this. She already knew how to keep her mouth shut, keep her thoughts inside. Now she was learning how to focus those thoughts into a particular kind of rage.

She also learned how to fold napkins in the shape of swans and fans. And she learned how to carry large trays loaded with hot plates flat on her palm. She would glide elegantly through the spacious main dining room, stare out through the wall of windows at the view of the golf course she wasn't welcome to visit, and never drop a thing. She never spilled when refilling water glasses and coffee mugs, as much as she would have liked to sometimes, right on their spoiled laps. Instead she totaled bills quickly and got people out the door so that they could enjoy their day on the links or at the pool.

Have a good game, she would say. Don't forget to use sunblock.

She was also instructed to memorize everyone's names so that she could greet them properly. Hello, Mrs. Pollack. Good afternoon, Mrs. Greenhill. Iced tea, Mrs. Hornstein? She was horrible at this, but they never remembered her name, either, and she was the one wearing a name tag.

Her boss, Eugene, noticed her poor memory, and called her into a meeting one day after her lunch shift. Eugene terrified her. He always put his arm around her and acted like they were buddies, but deep down she knew he hated everything about the country club, including the people who worked for him. At any moment he could turn on you.

He had a shaggy porn-star mustache and wore three-piece suits in crazy colors like maroon and honey. He thought he was psychic. He always asked everyone what their sign was and when they told him, he would say something like, "You are *such* a Scorp!" He claimed his boyfriend was psychic, too, so look out, world. Maggie wondered if they even needed to utter any words out loud at all when they were together, or if they just sat there, reading each other's minds.

In his office, he was gentle with her.

"Not everyone has that skill set. You have other talents," he said.

Maggie pictured herself shaving off his mustache with a straight razor. She was nicking him, and blood was slipping forth from his skin and dripping down his face in tiny droplets.

"You are charming and have a lovely smile. And I've noticed when you calculate the checks, you do most of the math in your head. That's very impressive. Not everyone can do that. We *definitely* don't want to lose you. So this isn't a warning or anything, just a suggestion. If you're not sure of a member's name, just say 'ma'am' or 'sir' instead."

"Thanks for the feedback," she said, lying, lying, lying. Being the nicest girl in the world. "I just want to do a good job."

But even though it wasn't a warning, he asked her to switch a few of her shifts to breakfast instead, which meant she had to get there at 6:00 AM instead of 10:00. It was obvious someone had complained.

Probably Mrs. Pollack. Her husband was the frozen-food king of the Midwest so she thought she owned the place. Maggie never forgot her name, but once had mixed up Mrs. Lowe with Mrs. Kahn, both of whom were Mrs. Pollack's best country-club girlfriends. They all ordered the same egg-white omelets and side of fruit for lunch every day, wore the same light cotton windbreakers in varying shades of pastels, and had the same hair, short and puffy and vaguely thinning, so that their skulls shined through in the afternoon sunlight. They took turns sending their food back, every day a new problem. The egg whites weren't cooked enough. The egg whites were cooked too much. Are you sure these are egg whites?

You try telling them apart, thought Maggie.

It was probably best that she get out of the lunch shifts. She was starting to fantasize about putting razor blades in the food.

YOU WANTED to kill them?

I wanted to wound them.

I just don't believe you, he says. You don't have a mean bone in your body.

Oh, I'm sure I have at least one, she says.

———

THE FIRST FEW morning shifts were bliss, so different from lunch, quieter and faster. There were only men in the mornings, trying to catch a game before they went to work. They would come in, sometimes in pairs, sometimes alone, and consume their breakfast hurriedly, as if the plates would be taken away if they didn't act fast. Maggie liked watching them as they hunched over their *Wall Street Journals*, imagining how snotty and shrewish their wives were, how spoiled their children would be acting if they were at home right now. This was their only escape, and they counted on Maggie, young, fresh Maggie, with the freckles and the sleepy eyes; a pretty little college girl, to provide them with peace and comfort.

This is where she belonged all along.

Maggie enjoyed her new schedule, too. She looked forward to going to sleep directly after dinner and getting up at 5:00 AM, every day, to feed her men, breezing past her father's entreaties to play Scrabble with him, or at least watch the news with him, pass a little time, fill a void, before he left to go out with the newest student who was spending several thousand dollars for the privilege to get drunk and sleep with him that year.

There was always one who caused a big scene at the end of the summer, drank too much at a party and threw a drink on him, or proclaimed her intentions to follow him back to California. In the past few weeks there had been regular hang-ups on the phone when Maggie answered, a game she used to play in high school, and Maggie wondered if her father were dipping a little young this year. But then she saw her one night, picking up her father on the street outside their house, a woman just slightly younger than her own mother, but completely different, lush and blond and hippy, with pink-tinted lips. She wore sunglasses on her head even though it was pitch-dark, and her skirt was too short for her plump legs, and when she saw him she grabbed his arm and then intertwined hers with it. They shuffled off together slowly, linked, and she laughed immediately and loudly.

Looks like they'll let *anyone* into this program, thought Maggie.

And then Joey Pollack Jr., husband of Miriam Pollack, father of Tyler and Amanda Pollack, son of that awful Mrs. Pollack, and heir to the Pollack frozen-food fortune, took his annual month off for the summer (He had an annual vacation for every season) and decided to spend every day of it at the club. He became the wrench in her plans for a serene summer. A big, noisy, shiny wrench.

He sat himself in the center of the room, the center table, every day. He was tall and tan and slender, and had an amazing crown of hair around his shining bald head. His teeth were huge

and white like a movie star's. His voice boomed like he was an-
nouncing a baseball game; it was impossible to ignore him. And
every day, every morning, he talked about blowjobs with his golf
partner.

"The wife and I rented *Truth or Dare* last night. Have you
seen it? Have you seen what Madonna can do with a water
bottle? The woman's got talent all right, but forget her singing."

"First date, I got a fantastic blowjob from my wife. Second
date, also a great blowjob. The third date I asked her to marry
me, and I never got head again. What's up with that?"

"All right, I got one for you, buddy. What's the best thing
about getting a blowjob from an Ethiopian woman? You know
she'll swallow. Get it? She'll swallow!"

Now him, she thought, I could cut.

The worst part was how he followed every comment with a
winning, glowing smile, and sometimes a wink, too, to let her
know it was only a joke, that she was in on it, too. He was only
kidding with the constant cock talk, he was really her friend.
Weren't the rest of these guys duds? Wasn't he the only one worth
knowing? And wasn't he the only one in this whole snotty place
who recognized that she was alive? She was oddly attracted to
him, too, even though she knew he was a lech and a perv, and
probably a philanderer.

"What's your deal, Maggie?"

He was eating his eggs, scrambled and runny, and a piece of
whole-wheat toast, no butter.

"Mr. Pollack?"

She was topping off his buddy's decaf.

"What are you, a college student?"

"Yes," she said. "At Princeton."

"Princeton, whoa! You must be pretty smart." He looked up at her, swallowed his food.

"I do OK," she said. "It's a lot of work."

"I went to University of Illinois," he said. "Not as fancy as Princeton but you get a good education there. What are you studying?"

"English."

"English! You should be studying to be a doctor or a lawyer or something. What are you going to do with an English degree?"

"I could be a teacher, or an editor. Or a writer."

"Yeah? You going to write a book about all of us?"

Yes, that's exactly what I'm going to do, thought Maggie. I'm going to write a book about you. You and your friends and your blowjob jokes.

Maggie shrugged, let her lids drop down halfway, then dropped her chin to her shoulder, rubbed it against the raw polyester of her uniform. It was one of her patented shy-girl moves that kept people at bay. Look how delicate she is. Don't ruin it with too many questions.

"Don't forget us when you're famous, all right?"

"All right."

She heard him say as she walked away, "Cute girl," and when she looked back, he was staring at her like he would have preferred her to the eggs that morning.

After she had married the ketchup bottles and totaled her checks and unbound her hair from her barrettes, she walked home dreaming of Mr. Pollack. She imagined he was hiding in the trees, watching her, until she motioned to him to join her. And then finally he did, he was walking next to her, whispering filthy things in her ear.

AT NIGHT her father ordered another pizza and insisted she tell him about her day.

Maybe there's something interesting at this country club, he mused, his fingers to his chin. Maybe I could get something out of it. What are the members like?

Her father's books usually took place in testosterone-laden backdrops, like war zones or fishing boats, horse ranches or mountain ranges. *The End of Big Sky Country* was the title of his latest novel, which Maggie had yet to read. She started to scan the back cover but put the book back on the shelf when she read the headline, "Sometimes a battle for land is best fought hand to hand."

I doubt it, said Maggie. They're all into playing golf and being Jewish.

He was quiet after that. She knew he would be. Her dad used to be Jewish, but didn't like to talk about it. She had seen a picture of him from his bar mitzvah, hanging on a wall at her grandmother's house. He was wearing a yarmulke and a gray three-piece suit, standing behind a podium with a serious smile that displayed a mass of braces.

But then he went to college, started smoking pot for the next decade, and decided religion was the opiate of the masses. He became this numb mélange of academia, alcohol, and agnosticism, until all that was left in his life was a generic gift-giving winter holiday.

There is nothing interesting about any of these people, said Maggie. Trust me.

She knew she was lying, though. Joey Pollack Jr. had begun to mesmerize her. He was the center of her universe for forty-five minutes a day. She waited to see what atrocity would come out of his mouth next. Would he be sexist today? Or would his thinly veiled racism be making a visit? (He had a severe preoccupation with the length and width of the penises belonging to black professional athletes.) Or would he be showing blatant disrespect for the mother of his children today? He was so awesome. He was the most horrible man she had ever met in her entire life, and she was kind of in love with him.

The day he said the one thing he regretted about having kids was what it did to his wife's breasts ("Down to here," he said, his hands, palms outstretched, dropping to his waist), Maggie went to the 7-Eleven after work and bought a box of razor blades. She didn't know what she was going to do with them. I just want to hold them, she thought. I just want them in my hands. As she paid for them, she glanced up at the security camera. Captured on film. Some waitress in a cheap uniform, and her razor blades. She knew she wasn't doing anything wrong, but she felt like a criminal nonetheless.

Up the stairs, into the bathroom, she locked the door, pulled a blade out of the clear plastic box. She held it to her finger, she held it to her forearm. She pulled off her shoes and pantyhose and pressed it up against her knee, then foot, then calf. Flat silver blade against pink young flesh. The bathroom tiles were pink and white, and alternated like a checkerboard. She cut her calf, only a little bit, so there was only a little bit of blood.

This wasn't right. This wasn't her. She didn't want to cut herself. She wanted to cut someone else.

ROBERT HAS WALKED across the room. It's their living room, in their house. They live in Westchester, where Robert had always dreamed of living. Maggie has decorated each room lovingly. She loves to shop, and not just for herself, but for other people. She's what you would call giving. You want to make Maggie happy, just give her a credit card and let her go. That's what Robert always says about her. It's easy to make her happy. Let her give.

You're freaking me out, he says.

Good, she thinks.

You never had a summer where you went a little crazy? Where you drank every day, or you had lots of one-night stands, or you did too many drugs? Where you sunk lower than you ever thought you could? And the only reason you woke up in the morning was just so you could do it all over again?

I didn't want to kill anyone, he says.

I didn't want to kill anyone, either, she says.

Me drinking till I puked every night and sleeping with a couple of girls, who, yeah, I never called again, I don't know their names now, fine, I'm not proud of it, it's just not the same as slashing someone.

That was uncharacteristic behavior for you, she says.

Absolutely.

Well, for me, too, she says. I was not myself. I was someone else.

SHE STARTED CARRYING the razor blades in her pocket at work. She would finger the smooth plastic edges of the box when she would reach in to get her order pad and pen. Just a quick touch to make sure they were still there, that they hadn't fallen out and gotten away from her. She didn't want anyone finding her blades, finding out that she liked them, or worse, keeping them for themselves. It was easy to imagine her coworkers also wanting to slash up the clientele. The best you could hope for from club members was for them to ignore you. It was when they realized you existed that your life became miserable, because then you were there to indulge them. They paid a lot of money to have someone to order around.

"Hon? Can you top this off?" Joey pointed to his coffee mug one morning. "And can you take your top off while you're at it?" He said it in this very controlled voice, as if he were as entitled to nudity as he was to coffee. And then he followed it with one of his gigantic smiles and a slow, easy wink. Maggie looked into his eyes and held the look.

His tablemate, a vice president at his father's gigantic frozen-food corporation, almost did a spit take with his water, and then started laughing heartily. "Aw, leave her alone, Joey. Don't you know better than to mess with the girl holding the hot coffee?"

Maggie could feel every nerve ending in her body cutting into her skin.

"Anytime, Mr. Pollack."

Joey clucked his tongue and shook his head. Maggie imagined the top of his head was swelling and turning pink.

"Just give me some more coffee, all right, kid?"

Maggie poured his coffee, and walked back to the wait station. She filled the saltshakers. She bit at her thumbnail. She stood, she stewed, she waited. As tee times grew closer, a wave of heads checked their watches and then popped their heads up and made eye contact with Maggie. Then they drew little check marks in the air with their hands, or scribbled an imaginary bill on their palms, or mouthed the word "check" and raised their eyebrows. Maggie floated across the room, delivering bills to all the husbands and fathers who had come to her for sustenance. Three dollars, five dollars, ten. It didn't matter how much, there would be no cash exchanging hands, just a signature, an agreement to cover their financial responsibility. It almost made it feel like the meal was imaginary.

In the center of the room, Joey and his tablemate jawed some more, then slugged the rest of their coffee. Joey motioned for the check. His friend rose and left the table, headed for the men's room in the front lobby.

"You're being a little saucy today, aren't you?" said Joey, as Maggie flipped through her stack of checks.

"You're a little saucy every day," she replied. She found his check, slapped it on the table, held it there with her fingertips. "Aren't I allowed to play, too?" She tasted the tang of bile coming up from her stomach to her throat; flirting with him was literally making her sick.

"You can play, you can play," he said. He paused, then said, "See you out there," to another member as he walked past and nodded at him. "What time you done here?"

Deep breath. "Ten," she said.

"You want to go for a drive?"

Never get in a stranger's car. Was he a stranger?

"Sure."

At the end of her shift, Eugene caught her at the time clock.

"Maggie Stoner, in the office, please," he said.

His suit was light brown and his tie was bright bloodred and had little horses on it. All she could do was look at the tie. That tie sucked.

"Maggie, Maggie, Maggie." He tapped his fingers on his desk. "How do I say this? While I have heard only good feedback from the members as of late, I'm concerned you might be developing inappropriate feelings or relationships with some of them.

I watched you today, and it was like you were almost leering at them or something. And I don't know *what* you were talking to Mr. Pollack about for so long, but he's a married man, with children. We don't want people talking, dear."

Maggie sat quietly. How much she wanted to slice that tie right off his neck and stuff it in his mouth.

"Eugene." She stopped herself. "Eugene." She laughed. "Eugene. I really hate your stupid fucking tie."

And then she got up and walked out the door. She had only a little time to get ready for her date.

IT'S BECAUSE I said we should start thinking about having children, isn't it? That's why you're telling me this story, says Robert.

Yes, Maggie thinks. Why would I want to bring children into this world?

No, of course not, she says.

She twists the ring, the gigantic diamond ring, around her finger, loosens it from her flesh. Underneath is a white band of skin, one freckle in the center of it. A marker. You are here.

MAGGIE WORE so much baby pink lipstick it was all she could smell, waxy and sweet. She had rubbed some of it into her cheeks, too. Her hair was combed straight, the barrettes securely fastened. The razors were in her pocket. She had taken one out, and rubbed her finger against it as she walked through the parking lot, searching for Joey Pollack Jr. in a sea of BMWs.

Finally, in the last aisle, in the last spot, she saw him, snug in his front seat. He was wearing aviator sunglasses. He smiled when he saw her, unlocked the door, motioned for her to open it. When she did, a blast of air-conditioning pushed against her and a rash of goose pimples flooded her arm. A Phil Collins song was playing loudly; a ballad about star-crossed lovers, sung with earnestness. The car smelled like smoke. She didn't know he was a smoker. No, it wasn't cigarette smoke, it was too sweet for that. It was pot. Maggie took a big inhale, but felt nothing.

"Hey," he said. "How's it hanging, little lady?"

"Are you high?" she said.

"Why? You want some?"

"I was just wondering." She leaned forward, shoved her hands in her pocket, felt for the razor, stretched her hand down her thigh until her finger hit metal.

"This is kind of weird," he said.

"Why?"

"Well, this is my wife's car. Mine is in the shop."

Maggie squinted at him.

"Never mind," he said. "So what are we doing here?"

"What do you want to do?"

"I think you know." He rubbed his hand on his crotch a few

times, back and forth, until he was hard, the fabric of his pants stretching up toward the dashboard. "I want you to suck it."

"Let me see it."

He reached for his fly, unzipped it, and unfolded his penis. It was thick and dark, except for the bell-shaped tip, which was pink. "Come on, kiss it."

"Show me all of it."

He puffed up his chest, sucked in his stomach, wrestled with his belt. The sound of metal on metal. Then he popped open the button of his golf pants, hoisted himself up slightly, and struggled with his pants until they were down almost to his knees, the fabric bunched up underneath his thighs on the car seat.

His balls are so hairy, thought Maggie.

I'm playing for keeps, sang Phil Collins.

Hand in pocket, hand on blade, head to thighs, lips to thighs. *I'm in too deep,* he sings. Mouth bites thigh, mouth and head move up together, mouth surrounds him, takes it in.

"That's right, take it all in," says Joey.

Hand in pocket, hand on blade. A full mouth. Hand out of pocket, hand in air, hand on thigh. Flick finger on edge. Flick, flick, flick.

Then slash, not too deep, don't hurt him, just let him know, you're there.

Ding-dong, I'm here.

At first he didn't know he was bleeding, but then, oh boy, he knew.

"What the fuck?"

He pushed her head, and she hit the steering wheel. She pulled up straight, wiped her mouth, and then bolted out of the car, away, away, run away toward home, do it fast, do it now. She saw the blood for only a moment, a huge swipe of it, like someone had painted it on his thigh.

She made it home, running, a running waitress, she was certain she was a punch line to a joke. Through the front door, past the mirror in the foyer, and then she stopped. There was blood on her cheek. It looked kind of cool, but she wiped it off. Into the kitchen, where her father sat at the kitchen table, coffee cup to his right, *New York Times* arts section spread before him, the op-ed section waiting in reserve.

"Dad." She sat down next to him and began to weep.

"What's going on? Calm down, calm down." He put his hand on her shoulder and began to rub it.

"I think I'm going a little insane this summer. I'm being fucked up. I'm sorry."

He took her into his arms. "Shh," he said. "It's going to be OK. If there's anything I can handle, it's this." He smiled, he hugged her. His poor, pretty, crazy daughter. He was going to make everything better.

IT WAS ACTUALLY the only time he was ever cool to me in my entire life, she says. He got me a plane ticket to Europe and gave me a bunch of money. I went and found Holly and spent the rest of the summer backpacking with her.

Yes, a father helping his fugitive daughter flee from justice, says Robert; his tone ripens quickly to condescending. Very cool.

He didn't know I was fleeing. No one ever came looking for me. He just thought I was freaking out. And then he threw some cash at me to make it go away, and you know what? That really does work. You should know that by now.

You're mean, says Robert.

Only sometimes, says Maggie. And only a little part of me.

Let me introduce you, she thinks. Here I am.

THE MANZANITA GROVE

There are three things you need to know about Kong," Bill told Christina. "And if you follow them, everything should work out perfectly. First, don't ever look him in the eye, at least not now. He'll view it as a challenge. Wait till you get to know him first. It'll take a while, probably a month. But in the meantime: no eye contact. Second, don't touch him. He really doesn't like affection. Occasionally I'll give him a nice pat on the back, but that's me, and I'm the leader around here. He might nip at you or growl, so just keep your distance for the time being. And third, don't ever show fear to him, not for a second. Because the minute you do that, he knows he's won, and he'll bully you for the rest of the summer."

Christina eyed Kong as he was held by Bill, who while nearing sixty, was still fit enough to handle a 150-pound dog. A slight growl hovered in the dog's throat, as if he were on the verge of releasing it into a full-force bark. From the side of his mouth a tiny strand of drool dangled, also seemingly poised for something more disastrous. Otherwise he was a beautiful dog; thick, chocolate brown fur, golden around the eyes and paws, wide paws that reminded her of a lion's, and a determined snout. His eyes barreled deep into his head; two shiny black stones that looked like they'd be perfect for skipping.

"Aw, he doesn't look so bad," said Christina, and she reached her hand out to pet his head. Kong lunged forward, and Bill pulled back on his collar, his fingers digging into his palm tightly.

"Christina, please! You have to listen to what I'm saying. Kong is not to be toyed with. Got it?" He looked down, pissed off, and then up again with a smile. "I didn't mean to scare you, dear. I'm sorry. I just want this to be perfect for you."

"No, I got it. I got it. Don't look, don't touch, don't show fear."

"Oh, and if you can talk to him sometimes in a high, feminine voice?" Bill shifted his rich, deep voice into an imitation of an excited teen girl. "He likes that, I think. Don't you, Kong?"

Kong's tongue dropped from his mouth, and his ears perked.

"I can like, totally try," said Christina, imitating one of her Introduction to Comp Lit students from first semester, a young woman who always greeted her friends with an urgency and enthusiasm one usually reserved for wedding announcements or job promotions, not compliments on the color of a new blouse.

Kong barked at her, and Bill soothed him again.

"You know what? Don't do the high-pitched voice. Maybe he doesn't like it on you."

"No high-pitched voice. Check." Christina clenched the handle of her purse. I could make a run for it now, she thought. My suitcase is still in the car, and my backpack is right by the front door.

Bill pulled the dog out of the front room and onto the patio, next to a clear, chemically treated, full-length pool. He locked the sliding door that separated the patio and the front room, and mumbled, "You have to lock it or he breaks in.

"It's going to be fine, I promise. This is going to be just what you need." He put his hand to her face, ran his tan, spotted hand along her jawline, then up to her ear. He squeezed her lobe with his thumb and forefinger. "Allow me to give you what you need," he said.

As Christina leaned forward to embrace Bill, Kong hurled himself at the sliding door, savage noises splitting from his throat. He sounds like a monster, she thought, and held Bill even tighter, then looked around him at Kong and smirked.

THE DAY AFTER she started dating Bill Stoner—and everyone knew exactly when it started; they showed up at the monthly faculty reading series together, and Christina was wearing lipstick—people started treating her differently. She didn't mind it one bit. She didn't care if people thought she was sleeping with him to secure a position in the department (She and Bill had never once talked about her career. They had never once talked about her future at the university. They discussed only her thesis, a study of transcendentalism in the books of Louisa May Alcott. Bill was a huge Emerson fan and collected first editions of his books). Nor did she care if they thought she was seeing him because he was filthy rich from his books. (The first was still his most successful, a noisy novel called *Hanover's Last Stand,* about a harried husband removed from the life of his children by a controlling wife. He eventually stands up for himself and his independence as a man and takes his children with him on a wild cross-country ride, at the end of which he asks the children to choose between him and his wife. "Do you want a simple or complex life?" he said. "Have I not taught you to roar?" It became wildly successful after its embrace by the men's movement in the '80s. An only slightly more politically correct film version was made of it, where the wife joins them at the end of the trip, and she and the children embrace in the mountains as the sun sets behind them. The eye contact between the husband and the wife tells the viewer that there will not have to be a decision. They can work together for the sake of the children. Nick Nolte got an Academy-Award nomination for best actor, and there was also a nod for best adaptation. Christina saw it once in a feminist film-theory class during her undergrad days. Several of her classmates hurled objects—pens, wadded-up paper, and a tampon—at the video monitor as the credits rolled. Christina was embarrassed to wipe away a few tears at the end of the film, and kept her head down as she walked out of class.) And she didn't care if they thought she was impressed with his fame (a frequent talk-show guest, Bill reportedly played golf with Charlie Rose whenever he was in town).

She didn't care because she didn't think she was doing anything wrong. After so many years in academia, four years of undergrad, a misdirected master's in philosophy, four years of teaching at a private high school (sullen rich kids on better drugs than she'd had at their age), one year of culinary school, and then this seemingly endless foray into a Ph.D. program in English, she'd had enough crushes on older teachers—all unrequited for a variety of reasons, but mostly related to a long-term, long-distance boyfriend and a brief and highly unflattering lesbian relationship that haunted her through her early postgraduate years—to realize when she'd finally hit the fantasy jackpot. He could have been poor, untenured, and working at a small state school, but as long as he had wisdom and passion about his work, she'd be smitten, and Bill was well known as a top lecturer and an inspirational advisor. Rumor was, he had been thanked in the foreword of more academic books than anyone else in the history of the state of California. He's the grand prize, she thought.

So she ignored the comments of her colleagues, at the weekly gathering of the PhDrinking Club (Apparently even in our thirties we still need a club as an excuse to drink, she thought, but she went anyway), little nudges when they complained about tenured professors, for example, followed by a dramatic hand clamp on the mouth and someone whispering, "This isn't going to get back to Stoner, is it?" Her best friend at the school, Mandy, an associate professor in linguistics, had started adding the phrase "between you and me" as a preface to most of their conversations. Christina never knew how to respond, so she didn't bother. Sometimes she told him what other people said, the gossip, the criticism, because she wanted someone to share it with, and as the man in her life, he was the best choice.

And they had become immediately close; so many things about him soothed her: his low, warming voice, his tan skin, lined in ways that made him seem more interesting, the way he rubbed one shoulder when he had his arm around her, reassuring her that this was exactly where he wanted to be. It was as if he had no intention of ever letting her go, and it was like that right from the beginning. I'm his prize, too, she thought. So even though they had been dating only a few months, how could she resist when he invited her to his home up north for the summer? It was rash, certainly, and yet she said yes before she had the time to say no, a fact she had considered daily since she had agreed to go. But then she would think about having the time and space to work on her thesis and to do yoga, plus there was land, so much land he promised, a vineyard, a swimming pool, a hot tub (this was said with raised eyebrows because sometimes he was a little dirty), fresh air, trees, clear skies, dry hot days and cool nights, so many stars you wouldn't believe, and, of course, lots of wildlife, and there could be only one answer.

"I'VE PICKED OUT two rooms from which you can choose," said Bill. They entered down a long, dim hallway, lit only by a skylight that showed a bright blue sky and one slender branch of a fir tree across the corner of it. There were four doors in the hallway, two on each side. "Now I know it's going to be a tough choice." He started laughing, the only noise in the silent house. He laughed so hard, he had to stop walking, and he leaned against the wall for a moment. Then he wiped his eyes. "I'm sorry," he said. "I don't know why I find it so amusing. It's not." He pointed to the first door.

On the outside there was a small, painted wooden sign that said "May Sarton." Across the hall, on the facing door, there was another sign, which read "Edith Wharton."

"This house used to be owned by a couple, two women," he said. "It was originally supposed to be a bed-and-breakfast for women only, but my understanding is it turned into some sort of feminist-empowerment camp. So each room is named for a different female writer." He cleared his throat. "I just find it funny, being surrounded by all these women."

"I suppose it is a little funny," said Christina. (She might have laughed. She couldn't remember a few weeks later when she told the story to Mandy. Mandy had said, appalled, gasping, "Oh, my god! What did you say?" Christina told her she had said nothing, simply raised her eyebrows, and, "You know, gave him a look.")

"Anyway, these aren't the rooms I had in mind for you. Those are my daughters' rooms. For when they come to visit." He said this enthusiastically, as if it might actually happen, though Christina knew that that wasn't likely. Maggie and Holly, the mysterious daughters, hiding out on the East Coast, ignored their father most of the time. Even when he was in New York, they refused to meet him for lunch, or even coffee. He had confided this to her, moaned it into her shoulder late one night after a wine tasting that had gone awry. (He had bought two merlots and a burgundy, and then they had expertly drained them at his house, pulling out one bottle after another, as if their thirst were an illness.)

"They're grown now, they have their own lives, I understand. But a coffee? A fucking coffee?" He rarely cursed. It had shocked Christina, and she had pulled his head closer to her, stroked his head and neck with her hands, rubbed him tenderly. It was exciting to her, to see his sadness. She hadn't known it existed within him.

"It is my one failure," he said.

"Nothing about you is a failure. You're without reproach." She believed it, too.

He walked down the hall, and pointed. "I think you should choose between these two."

"Virginia Woolf" and "Louisa May Alcott."

"I thought either should inspire you," he said.

She opened the door to the "Virginia Woolf" room. Inside, there was a small, sturdy desk, with two small drawers, and a high-backed wooden chair that slid neatly underneath it. The walls were painted a deep red color, and they were blank except for a framed picture of Kong at play, his tongue happily hanging from his mouth, hanging squarely above the desk. There was a sliding screen door that opened out to a small trellis-covered patio, and a set of stairs that led up to a hot tub. Vines hanging from the trellis framed the screen door. A room of one's own, indeed, she thought.

"What do you think?" he said.

"I love it," she said, and she did. It was quiet, the light was fine, and the hanging vines made her feel like she was still in the middle of nature. It would be great for yoga in the mornings, too. She just needed some sort of reading chair, and a stereo for her relaxation tapes, and it would be perfect.

"Well, don't make up your mind before you see your other option." They walked to the other room, and Bill pushed open the door with a grand sweep. Inside was a sun-filled space, twice the size of the first room, painted a creamy yellow. There were two huge windows on one side, plus another screen door, and the ceiling was encased almost entirely in skylight; the room felt almost entirely transparent. There was a wide, antique desk with a full set of drawers, and a bookshelf next to it, each row full of thick, hardcover books except for an empty one, which was clearly earmarked for Christina's books. An oversized leather chair—its golden brown leather seemed like a pool of butter in the direct sunlight—sat in the corner next to a small entertainment center, complete with stereo system, television set, and DVD player. A stack of yoga DVDs perched on top of the television set. She picked one up and looked at the cover.

"I just bought a bunch, I didn't know what you liked," offered Bill.

Christina paused, read for a moment, and then said, "No,

these are fine." She looked up at him, bewildered, and then she burst into a smile. "God, of course. They're perfect. This is amazing. No one has ever done anything like this for me before." She hugged him, kissed him so fiercely that their lips emitted a joint smacking sound.

"And you can see my workspace over there," he said, pointing through the screen to an alcove jutting out from the house on the property. It ended next to a cherry tree. Kong paced beneath it. "So we can be near each other without, you know, being near each other. But we'll always know where the other person is. So we don't get lonely."

"Alone but together," she said.

"Never far apart," said Bill.

"THE TIBETAN MASTIFF is an exceptional breed," said Bill, his voice lowered even further, into what Christina recognized as the voice he used when giving lectures or readings. They were walking through the woods that filled out his property to the peak of the mountain. "They were bred for centuries as guard dogs, yet are still considered quite primitive because there aren't that many of them in existence. The female mastiff can breed only once a year, usually in the fall."

Christina ducked under a tree branch and felt cobwebs brush onto her forehead. She wiped them off with her hand, then rubbed it on her jeans.

Bill continued. "They simply haven't had the chance to

evolve in ways that other dogs have, and yet they're highly intelligent and independent. So yes, they're difficult to train, but I think Kong is worth it. He makes me feel safe—there are mountain lions in these woods, and they will attack. And I've always felt a distinct connection with him. I appreciate the challenge he presents, I suppose. But there can be but one king of the mountain, eh, Kong?"

"He's calm out here," said Christina. "This is the best I've seen him behave since I've gotten here."

"He's great on the leash," said Bill. "And I think he likes the idea of protecting us. That's half the reason I got him, because of the mountain lions."

"Could he take a mountain lion?"

"Absolutely. And they're all over the place."

"Good to know," said Christina.

They walked another ten minutes, Bill pointing out madrona and manzanita trees along the way, with their slick skin underneath the peeling skin, and various promontories where Kong insisted on stopping and surveying the woods. In fact he stopped frequently along the way, at a stray crackle of branches or a rustle in nearby bushes. It was a little tiresome, but Christina played along.

Finally the trees became shorter and sparser, and Bill announced that they were nearing the top. He directed Christina to turn and when she did she saw another mountain range, clear as day, facing them, and another one, hazier, to the south.

"It's beautiful," said Christina, beaming.

"I wanted to show you something." He carefully put his arm, slightly damp with sweat, around her and gently guided her north. "Do you see that, there?" He pointed.

"What?" She squinted.

"All those solar panels? That's Robin Williams's house."

"Really? Robin Williams. Huh. I enjoyed him in *Awakenings*."

"So did I," said Bill. "And the other one, where he dresses up like an old woman."

"*Mrs. Doubtfire*," said Christina.

"Yes, that's it! Fine work in that film."

They stared at Robin Williams's house silently for a minute, then continued up the peak. As they broke through a closed-in patch of bushes, thorny branches scratching against their shoulders and arms, Bill burst through labored breaths, "We made it."

Christina had to admit it was spectacular at the top. She turned and viewed mountains at every angle while Bill caught his breath, Kong dropping down next to him. The sky was a pristine blue, no clouds in sight. And the same trees she'd been walking next to for the last forty-five minutes, the ones that had huddled together as a team of branches waiting to poke her, had turned a rich, roasted color, and suddenly seemed exotic under the direct sun. She breathed in deeply and took in the sun on her face. Wrinkles be damned, she thought. Skin cancer, too. I just climbed to the top of a mountain.

"It's glorious, isn't it?" said Bill. "Come on"—he reached out his hand to hers and she took it—"let me show you around."

He showed her the stone circle formations surrounding a stubbly pine tree. "I think the feminists made them. Probably some sort of strange ritual," he laughed. Then he walked her to the land that bordered his property, separated by a fierce-looking fence. "I wouldn't touch it," he said. "It's probably wired." He pointed out a ghost vineyard, abandoned twenty years previous by a prominent winemaker. The quality of the grapes had just not been worth his time. He sold the land, and it had since been sold thrice over. The vines were unruly and sagging, and the rich green color, so prominent in Bill's vineyard, was absent, sapped by the sun and lack of water.

"And then this, now this is the best part," said Bill. He led her and Kong back up to the peak and then through some bushes into a grove of manzanitas. The empty space beneath the trees was small—they both had to hunch slightly—but wide, so they could move freely beneath the peeling trees and their out-stretched branches. They took a seat at the feet of a huddle of larger trees. Bill hooked Kong's leash to a branch, then shuffled over closer to Christina. They both leaned back on a trunk, and looked up through the crisscross of branches at the bits of clear blue sky etched between them.

"It's amazing," said Christina. "I'm so glad I came. I knew this was the right decision."

"Was there ever any question?" said Bill.

Christina smiled and looked down at the ground. "A big move is always scary," she said. "But I'm here now, and I'm not scared at all." She kissed him, and his lips felt warm and smooth, and then she kissed him again and she felt an urgent burn between her legs. She put one hand around his neck and another on his chest and began to kiss him quickly and furiously. She moved her hand from his chest to his shorts. "Let's do it right here," she said.

"Here?" Bill said, and he laughed nervously. "Probably an unwise idea. There's poison oak everywhere."

"I don't see any. Come on, Bill." She undid his fly, reached her hand inside.

"I can't right now," he said. His smiled right through Christina. "I'm tired from the walk." He pulled her hand gently away from his shorts.

"Well, then do me," she said. She stood and, back slightly bent, dropped her shorts. "At least make me feel good." She flattened herself against the trunk of a tree, then lowered herself to the ground. Nearby Kong lay patiently, keeping a watchful eye for mountain lions.

ANOTHER SENATOR had an affair, surprise, surprise, thought Christina as she watched Bill pack for his trip. Every time one of these guys got busted—this time a Florida senator with interests in the aviation industry, who had audaciously kept an apartment in D.C. for his mistress, a former waitress in a steak house popular with the Republican crowd—the talk shows trudged out Bill as an expert in masculinity and power. Christina slumped on Bill's bed, chin resting on chest. His schedule had never bothered her in the past, but that was before this summer, before she had been high up on the mountain, in the woods, alone with him and his dog.

Ah yes, the dog. She would be taking care of Kong while Bill was gone. At breakfast she had received typewritten instructions, detailing his food and exercise schedule. She reread it now, stopping at the final line: "Kong is at his happiest guarding something, so let him watch over you!"

Christina read the sentence out loud. "What does that mean exactly?"

"Just that he'll stick by your side if you let him. It's quite sweet actually. You could probably just let him sit outside your office. I shouldn't think he'll bother you at all. He just likes to keep an eye on things."

"I don't want him watching me when I do work. Or yoga." This seemed an obvious point to Christina. The dog was not to go near her unsupervised any more than necessary. Plus, she was in no mood to be watched all day. Wasn't it enough that Bill, as he had reported to her last week, could see the back of her head as she worked?

"Aw, just let him, Christina," said Bill.

Christina folded the piece of paper in half. "He goes in the vineyard for the day. He'll have plenty of room to run around, and I'll get my peace and quiet. He'll be fine."

"If you feel that strongly about it," said Bill. His voice registered slightly off-key.

"I do."

"Fine then."

Bill folded a white undershirt quietly, laid it on top of two pairs of fresh white boxers, and said calmly, "Can you at least take him to the peak tomorrow? So he gets a little attention."

Christina cocked her head, squinted at an imaginary point in the ceiling. It is these little moments, these little negotiations, that compose the skeleton of a relationship, she thought. Do I want the spine to be strong or not? She sat up straight.

"I'll take him tomorrow afternoon," she said.

AFTER BILL LEFT, limousine door slammed tight, a sharp sound that cracked the quiet mountain air like a gunshot, Christina realized it was the first time she'd been alone since she'd arrived. They slept together, ate together, hiked together, drove into town together, down the precarious winding road past hidden homes and wide patches of vineyard, Bill whipping around the curves so quickly it made her carsick. Even when she was working in her studio and Bill was working in his office, they were separated only by windows and screen doors and the ripening cherry tree, tiny stems dangling like Christmas-tree decorations.

"I can see you so clearly," he had told her.

She quietly padded through the front room, passing and

then returning to Kong, who rested out near the pool, restrained by the sliding door. She checked the door once more to make sure it was locked. He lifted his head, eyed her, then rested it down again glumly.

Alone at last, she thought. She flashed on herself as a teenager when her parents left her alone for a weekend. I should throw a party, she thought. And then, just as when she was a teenager, she realized she didn't have anyone to invite. Except for maybe the mountain lions.

Maybe I should look through all of his things, see if I can uncover a cache of stocks and bonds for me to pocket and then flee. Maybe there's a stash of dirty photos or a stack of love letters, some hidden insight into a dark weakness curdling inside of him.

But she was afraid to touch anything. Everything was so carefully designed and organized in his castle, pristine and tailored, then dusted enthusiastically by the Salvadoran house cleaners he employed weekly to clean his home. Lush suede couches snaked through every room, paired with inviting overstuffed chairs and matching ottomans, the perfect setup for reading and relaxing. The walls were covered sparingly with art, but all of it was original and signed, mostly landscapes, the great outdoors, hills and lakes and ridges, regal sunsets that crowned oceans and mountains.

More prominent were larger photos on his walls of him and his friends—famous ones, some of them—she recognized a few, while the pictures of his daughters when they were little, and a few of them as teens, and some older people—his parents, she presumed—hovered near bathroom doors and light switches. And then there were his glorious bookshelves, a king's ransom of literature, all separated by type, novels on one, collections of short stories on another, books he'd contributed to, books he'd edited, the classics, the work of his students, and one small creaky shelf weighed down with his remainders, extras sent by his publisher that he'd taken to readings and had never been sold. He had encouraged her to take whatever she liked and read them, fill herself up with words.

She didn't need to uncover any great secrets about him. Whatever he had done before her, it didn't matter. And she probably knew it anyway. After all, she had read most of his books.

Christina decided to use the time alone to do her work, consume herself even further with her thesis. Here she was in Alcott's ideal environment, as she was raised to be by her father and his friends, in the thick of nature. I am here for a reason, thought Christina.

She entered the long hall that led to her studio, determined to fill the day with Emerson and Thoreau and Alcott, last names that needed no firsts, names that shaped her entire world. She stopped herself in front of the Edith Wharton room, the safe haven reserved for one of Bill's daughters. I could just take a look, she thought. That wouldn't disturb a thing.

Inside, the room was simultaneously spare and glorious: surrounded by calm gray walls, there was a massive bed, intricate swirling flowers carved into its wooden headboard, covered with a rich display of bedding, serene lavender colors, stripes and flowers, a half dozen pillows arranged neatly as icing, a few with sparkling beads as a fringe; and a magnificent oak desk—an antique, Christina imagined—with thick claw legs, and a busty carriage, so long it almost stretched the length of the room. On a gentle brass nightstand sat a framed photograph of a younger Bill, arms wrapped around his two daughters, the one with a sweet and simple freckled face, sleepy eyes, straight pretty hair curved around her delicate chin, was wearing a graduation robe; the other, rounder, with a dark stare and set, determined lips, had her hand in one end of a mass of long dark curls, as if she were about to twist a handful, as if she were holding on to it for dear life. And then, nothing else in the room, just a spray of gorgeous sunlight through the windows, and a heavy, healthy persimmon tree, its rich green fruits clinging upward, lingering outside the window.

Christina pictured him picking out each piece of furniture, considering the color scheme, how it might match his daughter's mood or sensibility. He gave her a desk worthy of royalty, thought Christina. It was better than what he had given her, as it should be. She suddenly swelled with a thick feeling in her stomach, a warm and pleasant wave that crashed, then nestled nicely into her.

She closed the door, smiling, flushed with emotion, then turned to the May Sarton room. Inside, the room was much darker, though not grim, just wanting, waiting for the sunset. And then there was the bed, the same beautiful bed, and the bedding, pink this time, but the patterns were the same, the pillows dripping with beads arranged almost identically, the same brass nightstand, this one with a nick on top, perhaps from a careless delivery man, the same picture frame, the same secret smile paired with a serious one, surrounding a deliriously happy and, on further inspection, potentially deluded Bill, and the exact same desk, no heirloom, no antique-store find. She opened a few of the drawers. A receipt from Pottery Barn sat in one. She rubbed her hand on top of it. It felt slick and new. It smelled like fresh paint.

The swell inside of her dissolved like salt in water. One pinch, and then it was gone.

THE PATH to the peak was marked with strips of yellow tape, reminding Christina of trees turned into tributes for missing soldiers. Kong had taken an early, commanding lead, so they were walking at a brisk pace, but every so often, Christina would spot a yellow flag and think of men in uniform, making stirring speeches before heading into battle. What if this were a forest of soldiers? What if I were crossing enemy lines right now?

Kong quickened his pace, jerking her forward, as if he knew she was daydreaming. He sniffed the earth as he walked, but in a busy and self-important way, so that it appeared as nothing more than a glance at the world around him. As the trail grew steeper, his tongue dropped from his mouth, and he began to pant loudly. He didn't slow, though, skipping all of his usual stops at the promontories. He wouldn't rest until he reached the peak.

Christina tumbled after him, calling his name, begging for him to slow down. She tugged on his leash, finally digging her heels in the ground, and he stopped. "Let's just stand here for a second," said Christina, and she breathed deeply. "Come on, you bastard. Yes. Just stand still." She stared at the trunks of the trees, and then lifted her head to gaze at the nest of leaves suspended above her. The woods were silent, except for the sounds of her breath and that of the dog, and general forest noise: tiny bugs buzzing, the wind in the leaves, an occasional chirp of a bird.

And then there was a crunch of leaves, footsteps perhaps, off in the bushes behind her. She heard another rustle, turned, and saw a group of birds taking off quickly in the sky, their delicate wings fluttering in fear. Her heart began to pump even faster. Kong stood, and crossed behind her. He didn't pull on the leash, but he stood there, alert. He sniffed at the air, and then he inched forward. He looked back at Christina. There was another crash of foot to leaves, and then, slowly, another. Kong let out a bark, and then there was a mad moment, where Christina could have sworn she saw a deer, but it was just for a second. It was definitely an animal, though, off in the trees, and it had heard Kong, and it was scared. Kong pulled on his leash, but the noise drew farther away, until the footsteps became one with the other sounds of the forest, and they knew they were alone again.

"Good boy, Kong!" she said.

He turned his head back at her, and looked her directly in the eye. She reached her hand out tentatively, and thumped his back with her palm. Her voice skipping, she said, "Oh, OK, there you go." She laughed a little bit, and patted him once more. "Yes, good, yes."

WHEN BILL RETURNED from his trip later that night, he found Christina sitting on his favorite chair in the corner of the living room, a copy of his second novel, *On the Emperor's Ridge,* in her lap, and Kong at her feet. He jumped up when Bill entered the room, raced around him, then after a few pats, loped back over to Christina's feet, and sat.

"What's going on over here? Did we make friends?"

"We made friends," she said, and recounted the incident in the woods.

"I can't tell you how much this pleases me," he said.

"I feel like everything is going to be fine now," she said. "I think he just needed to save me."

"He truly is a king among dogs," said Bill.

"Well, I don't know about that, but I do know that he's a good boy," she said, and patted Kong's rump.

"OVER HERE," said Christina. "That's where I saw the deer." They were heading back up to the peak again, so Bill could see where the actual bonding had occurred. Bill had insisted on getting up the next morning, as soon as the sun rose. He said it was because it would be cooler earlier in the day, but she thought he seemed a little restless, and, frankly, jealous at how close Christina and the dog had become in just one day.

"You're always going to be the leader of the pack," she assured him. "I'm just the damsel in distress." It amused her tremendously that this dog saw her as weak and defenseless. But she had to admit she was glad he had been there, even though it had been just a deer.

"That's the spot," she said, and pointed.

Bill and Kong stood there, both peering into the bushes, as if they could uncover some great mystery of the universe with the force of their vision. My heroes, thought Christina. She walked up the trail ahead of them, near a pair of manzanitas, and leveled her footing on a small space of flat land. Behind her she heard them traipse into the bushes, and the crisp noise of their feet on the leaves. What does he think he's going to find in there, she thought. Deer shit?

Christina placed her hand gently on one of the trees. Kong let out a bark, and she heard Bill hush him. She began to finger the peeling trunk, scraping off small bits along the way. As she watched the skin flutter to the ground, she felt extremely satisfied. It was as if she were tidying up the tree. Grooming it. When I am done with this tree, it will be the most perfect tree on the mountain. I can make it work. I can make it happen.

There was a rustle, closer to her, and she looked up the trail, past a trail marker, past a mess of shrubs, till her gaze arrived at a mountain lion, the eyes in his squat head glowering at her above his slender frame, his long tail cutting calmly through the air. Christina jumped back, and fell into a tree. She felt her head collide with something, a branch maybe, and it stung deeply. She sunk to the ground. "Bill!" she yelled. "There's a mountain lion!"

"I can't hear you," she heard back.

"Bill, there's a goddamn mountain lion!" she screamed. She met its golden eyes. It still hadn't moved.

Suddenly Kong came running out of the bushes and up the path, Bill following a moment later. Kong took a moment to make eye contact with the other animal, and let out a low growl. Bill stood back away from the two animals and Christina. Kong began to bark, and then burst up the trail toward the mountain lion, who turned and ran. The dog followed him into the bushes. There was a tumble of noise, and some moans and cries of an animal, and then the rustle of leaves. Bill gingerly walked to Christina and leaned down next to her. She put her hand on the back of her head. It felt sticky. "I think I'm bleeding," she said.

And then Kong emerged, triumphant, from the bushes, and Bill stood.

"Did you get him boy? Did you get him good?" He strode over to his dog. "Holy shit, did you see that, Christina? He took him. He fucking took him." Kong gave a mighty shake of his head. "That's why I have this dog, for exactly that reason." He slapped Kong's back, ruffled his head. "Yes, Kong, good dog. Yes, you are." He pulled his hand up and examined it. It was red. "He got you a little bit, didn't he, boy? But I bet he looks worse."

Christina hoisted herself up on the manzanita tree, the flakes of trunk falling under her fingertips.

He turned back and smiled at Christina, his cheeks burned with red. "Did you see him, Christina? Did you see what my dog did?"

AFTER SHE GOT out of the hospital (eight stitches, not that Bill would know; he spent the day at the vet's office while Kong got a series of painful shots), she headed straight back to school. Mandy would put her up. Mandy never liked Bill. She'd be the first to listen when she talked about how he loved his dog more than her, told her how to talk and act and walk, how he'd given her typewritten instructions on how to deal with a dog, how he'd watched her like a hawk when he wasn't off being famous somewhere, how he was slowly closing in on her but only on his terms, only when it was convenient for him, how he almost got her, she was this close to falling for it, how all the little things she liked about him in the beginning were all the things she hated about him in the end.

HE GIVES PAUSE

I see you, beautiful you, walk in the door, and a simple, potent pain strikes me in my chest. I would like to ask that woman to dance, I think. If I could I would. But your eyes are pointed south, like you're not looking for any company (or trouble), just a quiet night out, you and a drink. So I decide not to intrude on you and whatever thoughts might be fighting for your attention. I know what that's like, the fighting. Instead I drop two more quarters in the pool table, rack 'em, and start yet another imaginary game with myself. After I've sunk all the stripes, I order another pint. As I'm leaning on the bar, chalking up my cue, checking out my next shot, that's when you finally notice me, that's when you speak to me for the first time.

"Nice night, isn't it?" you say, and I say nothing.

You've heard of pauses, right? People use them for dramatic effect in speech a good percentage of the time, and then there's that small sect of people like me, where we're pausing because we're thinking of what to say next. And in that time, a million thoughts zing through our heads, until we are ready to pick through them all to find the exact right thing to say. Sometimes even more than a million.

"It sure is," I say. "We got lucky this year. Indian summers are pretty rare."

"It's my first fall out here. Out west. I was afraid it was going to be raining the whole time." Your head is down when you begin to speak, and then your neck rolls to the side, slowly, brushing against your shoulder, like you are stirring from an afternoon nap; and the words roll with you, with your neck and head, your hair brushing your bare freckled shoulders, until finally I can see your face, that your eyes are still sleepy, that the freckles on your shoulders match the freckles on your cheeks; and then at last, when your eyes are wide awake and meet mine, it's as if you've just taken my hand and held it. "But it's been lovely," you say.

Most people I meet don't know how to wait for the next sentence. They think I'm ignoring them, or judging them. Or that I'm shy. Or that I'm slow, which I am, but not in the way that you're thinking. They'll turn their head after the first ten seconds, start talking to someone else, or look over their shoulder to see if there's something distracting me. It unnerves people. I know it.

"New in town?"

I motion to the stool next to you, raise my eyebrows. You nod. "Please," you say. I settle in, balance the cue against the bar, drop the chalk next to my idling pint glass.

"New, yes," you say. "Everything is. New, I mean. New job. New apartment. New life."

My mother (unofficially) clocked my longest pause at a full six minutes in 1986, after she asked me if I had taken out the trash. I had, in fact, done it, but I just couldn't remember, and then this song came on in my head, and I was off. I think it was something off of Rush's *2112*—I had been making my way through a stack of albums my older brother had left behind when he went off to college—and all those songs were long as hell. During those six minutes my mother grounded me twice, and almost slapped me. This was when I had just started pausing. My parents thought I was stoned throughout most of my freshman year of high school because of it.

I pick up the glass, examine the rich red jewel color of the beer. Then I take a studious sip, a long one, like I'm trying to get drunk, which I'm not. I hope I don't give you the wrong impression. "Where you coming from?" I say.

"Back east. New York. Westchester."

My parents took me to all kinds of doctors in Portland after I started pausing: speech therapists, pediatricians, psychologists, psychiatrists (I can never remember the difference between the two, only that I needed to see both), and even a neurologist. The CAT scan scared me, and the psychiatrist (or was it the psychologist?) put me on so many meds I used to cry at night, when I wasn't so numb I was staring into space. I begged my parents to let me be.

"I'll talk faster," I said. "I'll try."

Finally we went back to where we started, our family doctor.

"Maybe," he said, "he's just *thoughtful*." And for some reason, that seemed to satisfy everyone. In a way, I was the opposite of dumb, although I wouldn't necessarily call me smart, either.

"So how'd you end up out here? Most people you meet in this bar either grew up here or go to the art school in the next town. Tell me you're not a first-year sculpture student."

You laugh. Oh, you have a charming laugh. It's thick and hearty. Your laugh is blowing my mind.

"That's sweet of you to say. My undergraduate years have long since passed. Want to see my ID?"

I laugh back at you. That I can do, no problem. Laughing is easy, though I don't find much funny. I'm picky, I suppose. I hold my hands up, palms toward you. I give, you win. You're no college girl.

"I got divorced."

You drop your eyes to your hands, an imaginary ring still lingers on your finger. There is a delicate white line still wrapped around it, a final reminder you'll have for a while. And in the center, the perfect center, is one perfect freckle.

I'll bet you had a big old rock. I bet you made him treat you right. You seem a little fancy. Your hair is cut nicely around your chin, your skin glows like the moon on a clear night after a good rain. You look like you've been taking care of yourself, like you've had the time to take care of yourself. Most women I've met around here don't even know they're supposed to take care of themselves like that. Or maybe they've just got better things to do with their time. I'm not judging you, though. You're just different is all.

"And then I had to work again. So I got my old job back, but they could only place me out here. Just for a few years, they said. But I'm glad. It's good to be working again. No, I really am. I forgot what it was like. To work."

I scratch behind my ear, I look down at my beer, I shift on my stool. Then, finally, grudgingly—it feels just like that, like my brain and my mouth are wrestling like brothers, and when I speak my mouth is saying "uncle"—I release some words: "I believe you."

"Plus it's quiet out here," you say suddenly. "I like it. I like it a lot. People seem to just talk all the time out east. Talking, talking, talking."

You put your hand in profile in front of your face, then bend your thumb against your other fingers like a pair of flapping lips. I notice the large diamond studs piercing your shapely, milky ears. There they are. There's what's left. It stings my eyes to look at them.

"It's like, enough already," you say. "Just be quiet."

You'd think it'd be hard for me to get by in high school and even college, and I'll admit my teachers stopped calling on me after a while, especially since the other kids loved me, saw my silence as a subversive act designed to throw the teachers off their perfectly timed lesson plans. I aced every test I took, though. As for making friends, well, I grew up with everyone I went to high school with, so they were accustomed to my pauses. Just as Ricky—now he's Rick, I know, but old habits die hard—Waterman added five inches and forty pounds his sophomore year of high school, and another two inches a year till he graduated, I added ten seconds, then twenty, then thirty, to my pauses. Now I average a minute, minute and a half most days.

The pauses are different lengths for different people. Like Ricky, I see him once a month, I go over to the house, hang out with him and Cindy and the kids, and I might not pause more than ten, fifteen seconds when we're sitting out back, drinking beer. We always talk about the same things, listen to the same songs on his boom box, and he always looks the same, give or take a couple of pounds, so there's nothing new to distract me. But when I meet someone new, someone like you, and you've got a new story, and such a different way of talking than most people around here—don't get me wrong, I like it, I like it a lot—it takes me a while to get to my next point. Right now, I feel like I've been pausing forever.

"I'm being coy," you say. "Sorry." You name the large software corporation close to Portland. Strategic thinking. Quarterly reports, 401(k). An office. A small one. But there's a door you can close, and that seems important to you. You say "three weeks vacation" like it's a mantra, then shyly admit "after the first year."

I drop a coaster, bend over and pick it up, wipe it off. "You landed south," I say. "Most folks just move to the city when they work there. Looking at you, I would have called city."

"I'm hiding out," you say, and you look over both shoulders like someone's going to come up behind you, eyes huge, eyebrows raised, long sweet neck extended, and it's exaggerated to make me laugh; you're kidding, is what you're telling me, only I know that you're not.

I pick up the chalk, fit the groove onto the tip of the cue. I check it twice, blow once. I act like it needs to be perfect, but really I'm used to all kinds of flaws. Everyone's got their thing that makes them stand out. A buddy of mine—I'm not going to say who, but if you live here long enough, you'll figure it out—he's on the meds now. His wife left him for some guy from Chico who came into town for a few months to teach at the art school. They'd only been married for a year, so I guess if there's any time to show your cheating colors, she picked the right one. Might as well get it all out in the open in the beginning. Anyway, the split really threw him for a loop, so I guess his dosage is pretty high, and it's been wreaking havoc with his digestive system. You'll be out on a Friday night, here, or at one of the restaurants downtown, and then all of a sudden he'll clear the room, it'll smell so bad. But do we stop being friends with him? No.

I'm sure you've got your thing, too, though it's hard to imagine it from just looking at you. I mean, you're a gorgeous woman—a woman, right, you're no kid, I was just playing with you—and everything about you is tripping me out. The way you speak is so measured and calm, like you're hammering in a nail with one clean shot. You're a working woman, that always impresses me. I can't tell you how many women are looking for a free ride around here. I need a woman who has her shit together. It's easier to hold your head high and stand up straight when you've got somewhere to go in the morning. Spring in your step as you walk out the front door. I bet you've got that spring. I'll bet you're going places.

Plus you've got that pretty red hair that falls so nicely on your shoulders. And those freckles, man, I want to start counting them, then lose track and have to start all over again. I want to hold your cheeks in my hands, stroke them gently with my fingers. Kiss the tip of your nose, then your forehead. Let your eyelashes flutter on my chin. Then take a big taste of those lips, top one, bottom one, both of them, suck it all in.

I don't meet a lot of women I like, so when I do, my heart practically explodes.

"You're safe now," I say.

For a long time I thought my perfect woman would be one who stuttered. By the time she had finished what she wanted to say, I would almost be ready to speak. And when I finally met a stutterer, a pretty design student named Sarah, right here in this very bar, I felt like everything in my life up until that point had been on hold, that now my life was truly ready to begin.

Sarah, she told me so many stories when we met, about being raised in a Christian family who prayed and tithed on Sundays so that they could yell at each other guilt-free the rest of the week. Three older brothers who told Sarah she wasn't loved when

their parents weren't around. A sweet chubby toddler crying underneath the back porch, drawing pictures in the dirt with her
finger to keep herself company. And then they told her that her
blossoming hips were fat, every day, every meal. There was a lisp
that turned into a stutter. And now she was dumb, too, they said.
So she took an overprotective pothead as a boyfriend, one who
did all the talking. She started to smoke a lot of pot and watch
MTV, stare at the rock stars with their big hair and wild makeup.
She would sing along to every song without the slightest stutter.
Their words were so easy to memorize. And then she turned to
herself, learning how to put on thick eyeliner and shiny lip gloss
and keep it perfect all night long, even if it meant running to the
bathroom to reapply. "I'm sorry," she'd said that night. "I'm always checking myself."

Almost every boyfriend since the pothead she'd met in a
bar, that's what she told me. Because it was noisy, because they
couldn't hear her stutter, because then she was unafraid to be herself. It was true, she stuttered less when we met that night, and I
could keep up with her conversation-wise. It was a lot of work,
and I pulled out every trick in the book, but I did it. Back at her
place we were silent as we groped and kissed. We never discussed
or questioned what we were doing, not when we took off our
clothes, dropped them into a sloppy pile on her floor next to an
ashtray filthy with cigarettes, not when we rolled around on her
mattress wedged in the corner of her bedroom, not when I held
her arms high up behind her head, one hand holding two wrists,

and kept going at her until at last, she hummed, just like anyone would. And when I finally came I let out a noise so loud and eager I, too, could have fooled anyone that I was perfectly normal.

But the next morning, in the silence of her bedroom, with only the occasional noise passing through—a bicycle rolling by as silent as a breeze except for the squeak of a chain, a bee trapped in between the window screen and frame, the growl of my stomach hungering for a hangover cure—when she spoke and broke through the quiet hum of morning sounds, when she stuttered, "I d-don't really do this s-sort of thing, you know," and listed off the handful of times it had happened before, it was like she was reading the *Encyclopaedia Britannica,* all the chapters, all at once. There was too much to process, and I became mute. Then she cried—"You think I'm a slut," she moaned—but still I couldn't get the words out. I got my clothes and headed out of her apartment, stopping only to stare at her sketches. She had faces all over the wall, portraits of folks around town, some of them I knew, some I didn't. I wished I had known her long enough for her to draw me. I saw her again only a few times—it's funny how you can hide in a small town—but it was always from far away, across the street, or passing by each other in traffic. Her face would flicker, a downturn of the lips, then head down and away. A year later, maybe two, she was gone. Good for her, I thought. This town isn't for everyone.

These days I usually get stuck with chatty women. They don't even stop to take a breath sometimes, that type. It seems like it would work out fine, but after a while you realize they talk so much because they don't care what you have to say. And I don't know, I think I've got something to say.

"So let me buy you a drink. One of mine." I'm a brewer, I tell you. They carry my lager and ale in the bar, and a winter brew is coming out in a few weeks. If you can let go of that vodka tonic you're gripping so tightly, I'd recommend the ale.

I'd be willing to bet I know more about beer than almost any man in the state, and that includes the beer snobs from up north who make it their business to try everything once, or the hobbyists in the suburbs, a sincere bunch of people who spend way too much time in their basements. My passion started in high school, where I spent a lot of time at parties drinking beer slowly as a way to pass the time during pauses. It wasn't so much the getting drunk part I liked as much as it was an acceptable way to make people wait for you to speak. And then I began tasting the beer, noticing the difference between good and bad, and wondering what went into it. College, I knew it wasn't going to be for me. I started out at the local brewery as an assistant, and then eventually I became the brewmaster. When the brewery went up for sale, I put some money together—my folks, Ricky, a few loans—and bought the place. Now it's mine, all mine. Well, mine, my folks', Ricky's, and the bank's.

I've got a small crew, and they work fast and quietly. Everyone knows what they're doing, no need for too many questions. We play music all day long. Most of the guys are a little bit younger than I am, so they bring in CDs of the newer stuff, and I like that. Keeps me young, even though I'm not really that old. But sometimes we don't play music at all; we just work quietly, side by side, getting the work done. Those days are my favorites, I think. There's something to be said for silence.

"Sure I'll have one of your beers." You sound delighted. "I'll try anything once." You talk for a little bit about needing to try new things. That you want to do more hiking. That you've heard there were hot springs around here, is that true? And finally, how your husband wanted everything to stay the same. Once you got married it was like your lives were over. Everything was locked into place. How close-minded he was. I can imagine you criticizing him, down to every last cell in his body. I know some women, they like to sting.

I bet you kicked his ass. I bet you destroyed him. Did he deserve it? Does anyone deserve it? I can see that you're merciless under that sweet, soft skin; that you can cut someone, that you leave scars. Did you fuck with him? Did you make him cry? I got it, lady. Now you get this: I am not afraid of you. I am not afraid of anyone. I'd like to see you try it on me. I already forgive you. Whatever you were before you met me doesn't matter, it only matters how you treat me now. Would you care that I left that poor girl alone in her apartment, all alone crying? Wailing. I could hear her down the hall. I could have stayed, I could have explained. I could have said *something*. I believe that we are the sum of all of the loves before us until we reach our one great love.

Whatever you did before, whatever I did before, we can put it all behind us.

"Are you OK?" you say.

I see you have figured it out, that my tricks have failed me at last. I want to tell you how I hear your words, and then everything transforms into something new, the sound of the letters separately and together, the intended and unintended meaning of the words, the sound of your voice, the tone of it, the expression on your face. Then there is the surrounding noise, overheard snippets of conversation, the clink the glasses make as the bartender stacks them on the drying rack, the country music playing on the jukebox, a sneeze, a cough, a door slamming. I have to process all of this before I can even utter one word in response. But I will save that for later. We have time.

Instead I say, "Yes, I'm fine. I just take a long time to respond sometimes. I promise you, when you get to know me, I won't take this long."

You say, "Oh, you're a thinker. Well, that's nice. I like it when people think before they speak. It means they're listening to you. And you know, there's something to be said for silence."

I take a deep breath, I nod my head over and over. I turn on my stool and face the bar, and you do the same. There's a mirror behind the bar, one below the shelves of bottles, another between the cash register and the wall, and we smile at each other's reflection. It's a punch in the stomach, love, but I'd take a hit for you.

INSTANT LOVE

The young stockbrokers across the hall are at it again, making sure everyone knows they're there. But, oh, how can we miss you? Every Friday night, every Saturday night, after the bars close, they're drunk and yelling, slamming doors, slamming them so hard the walls shake and it wakes me, every time, jolts me like an electrical shock right out of whatever dream I was enjoying. Or not enjoying. Sometimes I'm awake, up with whomever I've invited over for that particular night, and he'll say something like, "This is a real party building, huh? But I guess it makes sense, you're a real party girl." And he'll squeeze my nipple or palm my ass. Then depending on where we are in the night, we'll either do it once, hard and fast, or he'll walk out my front door, into the late, dark night, never to be seen again.

But right now I am alone, because there is no one new on any of the five Internet dating sites I frequent, looking for late-night play. It's just the same old desperados, dire men in their forties who wear ill-fitting oxford shirts and send decade-old pictures of themselves in a windbreaker on a coast, or from the waist down, cock erect; and then a handful of younger guys, stoners in shell necklaces who are just looking to smoke pot with a lady, and then either give or receive some form of oral sex. They know who I am and I know who they are. We're not interested.

And I am awake. I can hear the Wall Streeters laughing their bawdy, wild laughs. They say "dude" a lot; they use the word as a punctuation mark. At some point in the night someone will make a barking sound. If I were the kind of woman who made wagers, I'd lay a twenty-dollar bill on it. There is always a bark. Then there will be a fight. Sometimes they take it outside. Not outside the building. That would be too much effort. No, they just take it outside their front door. Next to my door. It's almost enough to make me want to find a new apartment. I'm simply not getting enough sleep.

They moved in six months ago, greased the building superintendent's palms with thick stacks of twenties, or maybe fifties, and nabbed that highly coveted three-bedroom apartment with the deck and the view (I've only heard, never seen). It seems like there are more than three people who live there, though, at least four, maybe five. They are all varying degrees of a youthful prototype that rejected me years ago in college—handsome in a way that comes from a balance of good genes, preferably of the Connecticut variety; smart, smart enough to get them through the day, to make their day better than that of most people on the planet; determined because they have been told to be so; entitled and confident; and just so fucking perfect. Now as a more mature and confident version of myself I can stick up my nose at them. I have slept with a few people like them since my college days, and their fetishes are boring. (Oh, you want to take me from behind and pound me like a racehorse? And call me a slut? How creative.) All the mystery is gone.

They are also a bunch of disgusting punks. They leave bags of garbage in our shared hallway for days, when it's not that hard to walk it down the stairs to the garbage room. And there are girls in the morning streaming out, looking like hell at 8:00 AM, ruining my morning coffee. At least I have the good sense to kick my men out after we're done. In and out in two hours or less. I don't pretend to be nice. I take what I can and move on. They should have the common courtesy to do the same.

The only one of them worth anything is the fourth—fifth? one of the extras, anyway—roommate. There's no way this kid is working on Wall Street. He's a shaggy, pretty thing with a slow shuffle for a walk, who comes in and out at all hours of the night, always on some sort of errand, getting a six-pack of beer or late-night slices of pizza, dragging a backpack stuffed with mystery items that bulge out the sides. His thick lips and strong jaw always seem to be working on something—gum, a cigarette, or the inside of his cheek. Not that you can see much under all his hair, a blond shag that looks gray under the dim lights of the elevator. But even though he keeps his head down, I know he's tracking everything around him. He's looked at me before, raised his head slightly, pushed his hair up, made that connection as he dragged his feet by me in the hall. I know he's on the ball, he's just undercover.

I'd invite him to play with me.

I REFRESH each of my five browser windows, squeeze my hands together, hard, like in a pissed-off prayer. My nails are ratty—I picked off the edges of the cuticles on the subway this morning, and I bit at my nails tonight at the computer, in between sips of a twelve-dollar chardonnay. (Good enough, but not great.) I should get a manicure, but I don't get manicures. It is so hard when you know what you're supposed to do, but then you don't bother doing it.

It's the same men in all the windows. Old, horny, stoned. I'm looking for the coked-up indie-rock boy who doesn't want to go to sleep yet and has tattoos on his arms of things that remind him how he's supposed to be in life.

This translates to "Be strong" in Swahili. This is the name of the first band I ever saw that made me realize I could get out of Oklahoma. She was my first girlfriend, and she taught me not to be afraid of love. I can't tell you what this means, it's far too personal. No offense.

None taken.

I would take a bartender getting off his shift, too. They're angry and edgy, and I like that. I have an itch I need to get scratched on nights like these, and disgruntled service-industry workers, they like to scratch.

All I see is one new guy with a *Star Trek* reference in his profile name, and then the rest of the regulars. They'd beg their case once again, if I let them. You won't regret it. I'll make you scream all night long. Let me lick you and please you.

But they have body hair in weird patches, or no body hair at all, and lumpy asses. And they're not funny enough, they have bad taste in music, and I sense that the little conversation we would have before we got to the sex, I would not enjoy. I used to think it didn't matter, but apparently I can't have anonymous sex with someone who isn't at least a little bit interesting.

I've tried it before, a few months back when I was first afflicted with this fever. This guy—my age, which is why I gave him a shot, thought we might have a little something in common—showed up in a peasant shirt and blue jeans that were like a second skin; 3:00 AM, and a peasant shirt. He sat on the edge of the couch, slowly unlacing his hiking boots, looking up at me, smiling, and I was suddenly shot with a volt of terror that he might actually say something to me, and that I would have to say something back.

He had curly hair that stood out from his head and a long thin nose with a tremendous bump on it. I wondered if he was Jewish. I actually have a thing for Jewish men. My ex-boyfriend Alan, the real-estate agent from Chicago, he was Jewish and had the nicest hairy chest. He would squeeze me all over and keep me warm. I need help with that. Keeping warm. If left alone for too long, I'll freeze to death. Maybe this new Jew could help.

And then as he squirmed out of his pants, I thought, well, it's winter, that's why he wore the boots, even though it makes no sense to wear something so difficult to untie if you're going to get naked, and maybe those absurdly tight jeans, those were the only ones he had clean, but at least he wore something clean, and that shirt, maybe he's an artist, or at the very least, artsy.

"What do you do?" I asked him. Looking for the tiniest tinge of attraction.

"I'm an accountant," he said.

When he finally got his pants down and shirt off, all that was left was an absurdly skinny man in atrocious tie-dyed boxer shorts, worn wool socks sagging around his ankles. If it were possible for my nipples to do the inverse of an erection, that they could somehow sink back inward, this vision would have surely done it.

But there it was—thankfully—a nicely sized hard-on. And when you are drunk, high on something new, and desperate, itching, needing to be scratched, you focus on the hard-on. It'll all be over soon anyway.

We did it on the couch, simple sex, my head and upper back on the arm, legs up in the air, and him on top of me, doing it simply, rhythmically, like fingers tapping on a calculator, adding one number to another, totaling it all up. I was silent throughout, I am almost always silent. He did it deep, which I like. He did it without variety, which I don't like. But you can't ask for much from a complete stranger.

When he stopped, he lay flat on top of me, and I let him catch his breath for five minutes. I clocked it, I usually give them ten minutes, but this guy, he had to go. He could almost depress a girl. I said, "So, thanks. That was great. Just great." He lifted his head. He looked like he didn't believe me. "No, really."

Why was I assuring him of anything? Why did I need to stroke his ego? I had every right to say, "You fuck just as I thought an accountant would." Not that I had ever thought about fucking an accountant before.

"It was just what I needed," I said. "But now you have to go."

He pulled himself off me. I pulled on a robe, tied the sash at the waist. He pulled on his pants, jumped up in the air to get the tight denim over his hips. I handed him his shirt, the flimsy cheap cotton scratched against my fingertips. He sat back down on the couch and slipped his feet into those goddamn hiking boots, and then, slowly, began to lace each shoe up. I stood there, hands folded across my chest, hands cupping my elbows, upper arms squeezing my breasts, a shelf of cleavage pushing against my robe. He double-knotted the laces. Come on, faster. Move it on out. Move it. Fuck.

Finally, shirt, shoes, coat, done. I walked him to the door and gently pushed him through it. He stood outside—why is he still here?—and then extended his long, bony hand for a shake. I had to shake it, this hand that had been briefly inside of me just minutes before. As I reached out my hand, nails bitten, I heard a pound across the hall. There was my neighbor, hair hanging over his face, trying to get in his front door.

"Good night," said the accountant.

My neighbor heard his voice, turned and spotted me in my robe, and then, gracefully, turned his head back. Respect, I thought. Or disgust.

"Yeah, OK. That's fine. Just go." I blurted it out, louder than I would have liked. "God, go already," I said, softer. And then he was gone, I was safe behind my door, and I thought: I'm really going to need to be pickier in the future or this is never going to work.

MY LOVE LIFE since I moved to New York from Chicago has been like a desert. I've had tiny little interactions of love, like finding shallow pools of water to drink from, and then I've moved on, hoping that I've stored enough love and affection and excitement to get me to the next place.

I've been stuck with a string of unsuccessful two-month re-lationships, the deaths of which have burned out almost all my romantic instinct and desire. I was in love with Alan, but I wasn't ready for it yet. I'm probably still not ready. But being who I am—not that I particularly know who I am, I just know who I'm not—I felt that I should keep trying for love. I mixed up the real dates with the one-night stands just enough to keep myself satiated. On the dates you did not fuck, in the bars you did. Those late nights at the bars, I recognize now, were just as much work as the dates: the talking, the drinking, the questioning, the laughing *so hard* at jokes that weren't that funny. They just never were funny. It's not funny, none of it, I know.

But back to the dates, the relationships, my flaccid attempts at legitimacy. Online dating has been the only way I've met men the last few years: nice, neurotic financial analysts, law students, and advertising account executives who made it perfectly clear they were ready to settle down every step of the way—in their ads, in their initial e-mails, over those first drinks in Chelsea, they were ready to go, if they could find the right woman. Are you the right woman?

I am not young anymore. I need to say that. Or I don't feel young.

Two months became the end point (if I could make it that far, but often I made it only a few weeks) because that's when the first (and last) big fight occurred. This led to a gentle fadeout of phone calls and e-mails, no holiday cards were necessary. Rarely have I had a big breakup, because at two months it's hardly necessary for any sort of scene. No one is invested. I can't get attached to anything in two months except for cigarettes, and I gave those up years ago. Those things will kill you.

But I am attached to sex. I get this from my father, who left my mother and younger sister and me twenty-odd years ago because we were seriously impacting his social life with his graduate students. Children can be such a drag, don't you think?

My sister, Maggie, and I would stay with him every summer in some rented house near the university hosting whatever writing program he was running that year, and try not to think too much about who he was or what he was doing while he was out with some nineteen-year-old, screwing up her head for the rest of her life. He would neatly stack a few twenties for us on the counter before he left for the night, enough to keep us occupied. Sometimes we would go to the movies; sometimes we would buy and eat so much ice cream—all kinds, Creamsicles and King Cones and Popsicles with gum balls at the center—our bellies would ache; and then sometimes we would keep the twenties and hang out and play backgammon. We never made any new friends (our father never bothered to encourage it; he didn't really have any friends either), it was just Maggie and me, entertaining ourselves and each other.

This was fine for a few years, and then suddenly it was not fine at all, at least not for me. (Maggie always loved those twenty-dollar bills. They were an adequate love substitute, like how some people feel about Equal in their coffee, ignoring any sort of long-term damage, like to brain cells or psyches. She even went so far as to marry a very rich, very chatty, very boring man, but she's since come to her senses and left him last year. Now she's shacked up in Oregon with a quiet man who makes beer for a living.) The last summer I stayed with my dad I screamed at him one night, blocked him from leaving, blocked all entries and exits with the sound of my voice: Why do you do this? Why? And he said, "When you're older, you'll understand."

I understand now. Because even when it feels bad, it still feels good.

It started slowly, this late-night sex life. It was after a bad date, one of many, they all blend together after a while. I went home, logged on to the dating site (I was using just one then; I've since cast a larger net), hovered my mouse around my profile, and then clicked "Play" in the list of romantic interests. I'd always just had "Dating" and "Serious Relationship" (never "Friends"— who needs any more friends?), and it had never occurred to me before to select anything else. But this seemed right, too, perhaps more right. Sure, I had slept with plenty of guys on the first date, but to connect with someone for just an hour, late at night, it was beyond slutty. By clicking on "Play," I was admitting that I was a complete deviant, that I just wanted to fuck. It wasn't about pleasure. It was about feeding very base and gritty needs. It was about being starved, being ravenous, and taking whatever I could get to eat. About wanting to consume. But there was no pleasure. I was required to do it, by what or whom I don't know. It was an uncontrollable urge. I had been bitten.

THERE IS A BLAST of noise through the walls, a thump of overturned furniture, perhaps a table, followed by the high tinkle of glass shattering. Then a body slams against the wall that faces my front door. Grunted cursing, and then loud squabbling, like chickens fighting over feed. Someone yells, "Enough!"

Yes, indeed. Enough.

Onto the couch, legs up, glass of chardonnay on the floor next to me. My living room is small (I've been meaning to find a new apartment since the day I moved in), and my couch is large.

This is where I have the sex. All my life I wanted a couch like this, a buttery soft black leather couch, big enough to lie almost side by side with someone, wrap your legs around them. Sink into it. This couch makes me happy. It reminds me of making out with my first boyfriend in high school. He had a black leather couch in the basement of his father's house. There was a tear in it. Sometimes I would finger the tear while he was in the bathroom or changing the music on the stereo. (The Smiths, always the Smiths. He would have traded me in for Morrissey in a second.) I would slip my finger inside of the couch. It felt soft in there. I swore someday I would have a couch like that, and now I do, but I rarely sit on it, just fuck on it.

Instead I usually sit in the chair by the window, feet up on the sill. I stare out at the building next to mine, the half dozen trees on the street below, spurting forth from the concrete, the fire hydrant, the double-parked cars, the deli on the corner, the one where the counter guy thinks I'm cute, but not fuckable. He told me this one night: "You look too wholesome," he said, "those chubby cheeks," and I thought, Brother, are you wrong. You don't know anything about me and my leather couch.

There are framed something or others on my wall. Pictures of pictures. Flowers, sunsets. A step above a dentist's office, a step below a therapist's office. I know I'm weak. I bought them because I thought I was supposed to. My true love is my book collection, that's why I rented this place. Built-in bookshelves, floor to ceiling, head to toe, stacked with everything I ever bought and never sold: biology textbooks from college and graduate school that I can't seem to sell or give away, so I hold on to them as a reminder that I am smart; collections of entire science-fiction series; books with faraway gnomes and fairies—it's weird, I know, but my sophomore-year roommate got me hooked on the stuff fifteen years ago, and I haven't been able to stop. I like going to those faraway lands; I like it when there are new words to learn, new cultures to understand, all vaguely like my own, at least metaphorically, but somehow different, more freakish, outlandish, whimsical yet dark. I reread some of these books at least once a year, take myself to that place again.

My books fill me. Just not enough.

AT LAST, a flash of fresh hope on the screen, a new message for me from a man on the Lower East Side who looks just like all the boys before him, young and wiry, sideburns like strips of bacon, long and unshapely, an inch of buzzed hair around his head, pulling back on his forehead in echo of a grandfather or a great-uncle, and two earrings in the upper right-hand corner of his ear. Two entirely gay earrings. But I know they're not supposed to be gay because, look right there, there on his profile, it says, "Straight," right above "Play." And I read his e-mail, which gently suggests that the red, red lips of my profile picture would look even better around the tip of his cock.

It's on. I am so troubled. And it is on.

I LIKE FINDING a new boy each time, I admit this. Uncovering a new treasure. And in the minutes between my sending him my address and his hopping in a cab and heading to my apartment, I am anxious and excited, as if I am waiting to hear about important, potentially good news. Not that I get a lot of good news these days. I don't get bad news, either. I am just treading water. Occasionally, on nights like tonight, I create my own news.

While I wait, I bite my nails, so raw and ragged, and then I realize I've been sweating for the last hour, chardonnay seeping out of my pores, and I've been ignoring it out of laziness. But now it's time to pretty myself for my latest suitor. In the bathroom I drop my robe to the floor, stumble into the shower, catching my foot on the curtain (I am drunker than I originally thought), and crank on the water.

Even though I shaved yesterday, I start shaving my legs all over again and under my arms, and while we're at it, why not hike up that bikini line? I soap myself all over, every pore, every crevice, scrub my face with a fancy grapefruit scrub my sister got me last year for Christmas, which I never use (She is always getting me things I don't need, spending her husband's money on products. God, so many *products*. She'll try anything once, or make you try it anyway) except when I feel like I'm supposed to, like on nights like this. I want everything to be glowing and pink, create a remarkable image for the man between my legs that night, so that he'll remember the experience fondly when he's jerking off a week later before he has dinner with his ex-girlfriend from college. Look how far he's come. He can get laid anytime he wants. With a pretty, pink, slightly older weird woman from the Upper West Side.

I also do this in hopes of some sort of karmic retribution, that he, too, is standing in a shower, perhaps a dingy stall in a shitty studio apartment, making himself nice and clean for me.

HIS LAST E-MAIL said, "Leaving now," an hour ago. He was supposed to take a cab. Maybe he took a subway. Maybe that's why he's late. He should have been here in a half hour at the most in a cab. There's no traffic this late. He would have come up Broadway. Maybe the West Side Highway.

I pour another glass of wine, the last in the bottle. Maybe it is the chardonnay. Maybe it has nothing to do with my father or my failed relationships or the isolation of urban life. Maybe it is just the chardonnay.

ONCE I LEFT a note for my neighbors. Their garbage was piled up two bags high, two across on either side of their front door, and the smell hit me every morning as I opened my front door. It was starting to seep under my door, too. I couldn't smell it all the time, but I knew it was there, hovering like an invisible force field. I was afraid one day I would wake up and be trapped in my apartment forever, a captive of irresponsible youth, a victim of mismanaged testosterone.

I tried knocking on their door, for a few days in a row, but they either weren't home or were passed out from a late night or a long day making money for people richer than themselves. I didn't want to be that neighbor who left nasty notes, so that when we saw each other in the elevator we could barely stand to share the same air while the floors ding slowly in front of our faces—counting off, when will this ride end? That seemed like something a cranky old lady would do.

But the smell: like old coffee grounds stuck in the filter, raw meat left out and gone bad, and dirty sponges on the day you decide to throw them away. It was the bottom of the garbage can, the corner where things catch and mold, every day in front of my door.

And then there was a pizza box, too, tiny bubbles of grease spotting the bottom of it. I imagined dried, old cheese stuck to wax paper inside the box. When they balanced the box on top of the bags one evening, like that last bucket atop a sand castle, that's when I cracked.

"Please take out your garbage," I wrote. "It smells. And it is unsanitary. This is New York! There are rats everywhere!" I underlined "rats" three times. I almost drew a picture of a rat, but I thought that would be too cute and I wanted to be taken seriously. "It is not fair to the rest of us."

I didn't sign my name, but a few hours later I opened my front door and the garbage was gone. My note had been returned to my door, and on the other side someone had written, "What garbage?"

I'M AT THE FRONT of my apartment, my knees clamped to my chest, head resting on the door, listening for hallway noise. It's after 5:00 AM. I think I've been waiting for two hours. I've just checked my computer; there's no one left online but a handful of men I've seen before, one of whom I dated briefly, and another whose profile name is MastaGangsta. I don't need a master. I just need someone who will show up.

And then I hear it: the elevator opens on the floor. He's here. He must have gotten in the building, he's sneaking up to surprise me. I knew he couldn't resist my juicy red lips, even if the digital photo doesn't do them the justice they deserve.

I stand up, brush myself off (there is dust on my legs from the floor), tighten my robe around me. Fingers through the hair, tidy those curls. I hear the footsteps come closer. Time for business. I open the door, light up my face, bite the inside of my lower lip to keep that light steady. Hold the door frame. Steady now.

I peer down the hallway. It's the one who shuffles, paper bag in hand. The quiet one. He'll do.

SO MY NEIGHBORS stopped talking to me after the note, cold stares at the floor in the elevator. They never hold the front door for me anymore when my hands are full with groceries. I am forced to drop the bags, dig my keys out, open the door, jam it with my foot, shove the bags inside, stagger on the street like a drunk.

Before that they had been pleasant young men during the day, even though they were crazy and loud late at night. All those parties they have. And they never invite me to even one of them. Not like I would come.

But still, it would be nice to be invited.

"I NEED YOUR HELP," I say. Blurt, like it's an emergency, which it is. Which it isn't. I want to reach out and grab him and pull him into my apartment. Kidnap him.

"What?" He looks up, pushes his hair out of his face. "Did we—did something happen?"

"I saw a rat. In my kitchen."

He looks disgusted, not at me, at the rat.

"A big one. Gray with a huge tail. I think he's under the sink. I could hear his tail knocking over bottles. Dishwashing detergent."

He tightens his hands around the paper bag he is holding. Looks behind him. His white moon cheeks and watery blue eyes made him seem frail and gentle, like he wouldn't know what to do with a rat if he caught one, that the rat would more likely know what to do with him. Just my luck. The late-night pussy.

"It would just make me feel better," I say. I suck on my lips. "I'm all alone in here."

He reaches in the bag, pulls out a can of beer, cracks open the top.

"Yeah, OK, I'll take a look," he says.

ONCE AFTER a big party where they made a dent in their front door, I left a note that said, "You are loud. You are the loudest people in the world. Why do you need to be so loud? Don't you know that other people don't like noise? Please shut up shut up shut up." Everything was underlined. Every single word.

IN THE KITCHEN I am teetering. The presence of someone else has suddenly amplified my drunkenness. I cling tightly to the counter, as if it is a life raft in the pit of a swirling ocean, only nothing is moving around me, not technically anyway. He looks at the cabinet under the sink, pulls everything out from inside, the dishwashing detergent (which stands, unfortunately, erect), an unopened pack of sponges, a bucket full of cleaning supplies, a container of old fabric softener I keep meaning to throw away but never do. He stacks these items behind him and then notices me and my grip on the counter. He asks me if I'm OK.

"It's the chardonnay," I say.

He shoves his head underneath the sink, really shoves it in there, and I stare at his ass because I feel that I should, but really, I don't even care what it looks like. He could have a huge backside, or no ass at all and I would still sleep with him at this point. He is there, and I am ready. I loosen my robe enough to expose the top half of my breasts. I slip a round, soft leg out from the silky fabric. Peekaboo.

His ass is small, as it turns out, like two saucers in a pair of jeans, and I bet it is rock hard.

He pulls his head out from under the sink. "Well, there's no rat," he says. "At least not any that I can see." He squats on the floor, takes a sip of his beer, squints at me. He bounces a bit on his calves. He nods at me. "There is no rat. Right?"

"Right. There is no rat."

"OK, so you wanted something else?"

"Right." This I didn't know how to do. Online, everything was already taken care of, fully explained by a system of clearly labeled and color-coded boxes. It was just a question of confirming the agreement. I stretch my leg out further, pull my hands up to my breasts and stroke the sides of them.

He looks momentarily terrified, and then relaxes. "Oh, I thought maybe you wanted to buy some weed. Because for that I'd have to go back to the apartment." He stands up and puts his hand on his crotch, starts rubbing it. "You want this though, that's what you want." He is hard in moments.

"Yes," I say. My voice is low and has edges to it. "I want that."

"You want to smoke some weed first? I could—"

"No," I say. "Let's go in the living room. On the couch."

"No, we're going to do it right here." He pushes me up against the wall, unties my robe, and heads straight for my breasts, takes huge tastes of them, bites them and licks them, as if he has been hungry all night. I just stand there, hands against the wall, letting him fondle and eat my skin alive. I am almost immediately ready for him to get inside me, but I sense that he needs to do this first.

"You smell good," he says. He licks and kisses down my stomach, gets on his knees and starts to bite my thighs, and then lick in between my legs. An involuntary noise rises from my throat and I emit it, it hangs in the air in front of my face, and then I release another.

"Fuck," I say. I put my hands in his hair.

He sticks a finger in me, and then another. "Yeah, you're ready," he says. He stands, slips off his grungy tennis shoes with one hand, keeping the other on my right breast, pinching the nipple. He is looking at me the entire time. He drops his hand to his pants, unzips, unbuttons, pulls them down over his hips and ass. "You still ready? Check to see." I stick a finger inside, and it is wet.

"I'm ready," I say.

And then it feels like it is over in an instant, if only because I wish it could have lasted forever. I am dizzy the minute he starts pumping inside of me. I wrap a leg around him and then my arms around him, and he mutters in my ear between thrusts about how he knows I always watch him, that he has watched me, too, that he has thought about my twat—*twat*, he actually says that—and what it would be like to fuck me in the elevator.

"Throw down your bags. Bend you over. Make you scream. Every floor. All the way to the top. Back down again. Fucking you."

I feel light like a child and I sink into him.

"You really thought that?"

"Sure," he says, and I don't believe him but it doesn't matter. I just let him rampage on for a few minutes. I am almost sleeping. And then it's over; he pulls out, jerks himself off for a minute, dribbles down his leg. I watch this, through a warm golden haze that has clouded my eyes and face. I feel hot, almost feverish.

"I need to sit down," I say. I pull on my robe, tie it tight around me, and then go to the living room. He pulls on his pants, grabs his can of beer, and follows me, rubbing the moisture off his hands onto his pant legs. I stretch out on the couch and he lays down next to me and puts a hand on my breast and massages it with his fingers, around the nipple, and underneath, where it's at its softest.

"God, you smell good," he says.

I thank him. He kisses me.

"You want me to hang out for a while? I don't have anything to do. I was supposed to bring the beer to those guys"—he motions his head toward my front door—"but fuck 'em. I can take a night off."

I didn't respond. I let my nerve endings unfurl from their tensed state. Calm down, children.

"I like your place," he says.

"Thanks," I say.

His hand picks up steam on my breast. "It's so clean." He moves his hand down my stomach, and I reach mine out and hold it there, intertwine my fingers with his. I am too tired to start anything else, but I cannot seem to say no just yet. "It's a real hole where I'm at," he says. "You could probably guess that, though."

"I could, yes."

He kisses me on the neck.

"Man, I'm getting hard again," he says. "I could get used to this."

I am flattered, I can't help it. I had turned him on twice. Maybe this is no fluke.

"You know I could come over again sometime. Spend the night. I could make you dinner. We could do this some more." He squeezes my hand.

"Maybe."

"Because honestly, I'd much rather crash in a place like this than with those guys. They're just a bunch of slobs. It's gross."

He shifts his arm up, and happily puts it around me. I picture a stack of garbage bags outside my front door, facing their twins across the hall.

We lie there for a while, our breaths catching in our throats, and listen to the distinct noises of the night turn into the roar of the day: an individual car hurtling through yellow lights, unchallenged; dogs greeting each other on their morning walks before their owners prepare for work; and the sound of a lone bus running the regular route, its breaks moaning for oil and tenderness at the stop below my window. Suddenly there is sunlight through the window, not a lot, because it's winter and nature is sparing with her love these months. Finally the streets grow anxious and full, the rest of traffic mixing with the sound of doors opening and closing, footsteps made by overpriced high heels and running shoes and scuffed dress shoes; everyone is shifting and moving at once, and the blend of the sounds and the piercing pure light through my window signal that while what happened between me and my neighbor was different from the usual, it is now over. I cannot go back, so now I must move on. I didn't know how this would happen, this progression, this growth, what form it would take, or how much work I would have to do to get there, but at the very least, I knew I was going to have to find a new apartment.

"So maybe I could stay here for a while," he says.

I look at him, try to picture him here in the morning and the evening, with the sunrise and the sunset, every single day. I can see someone, but it's not him, it's not his face. I see Alan's smile, and I see the legs of a man I invited to my house once, strong and lean, and I see a man with my father's mind, and I see a man who works two floors down from me at work who makes me laugh all the time in the elevator, and I see someone with my sister's generosity who can give until he bleeds—I like that sometimes, the bleeding—and I see the satisfied faces who look at me for that instant as they groan like I'm the woman they love. I see bits and pieces, parts, fractions, hundreds of people comprising the one perfect man, and I know suddenly that he's out there, even if this one, he's not the one.

SARAH LEE
WAITS FOR LOVE

1.

IT IS morning now, and Sarah Lee sits and waits for the bus.

2.

SARAH LEE falls in love every time she takes the subway, so she's started taking the bus instead. The L train from Williamsburg to the East Village is *killing* her, with all these cute young boys, with their lovely young skin and doe eyes and mussed-up hair, mussed up just so and their vintage-store winter coats, some military style, stiff and serious-looking, some more textured and glamorous, as if they should be walking the streets of London circa 1932; and all kinds of crazy kicks on their feet, expensive tennis shoes of vibrant colors, sturdy walking boots, and lately, cowboy boots with heels, but those are worn by the gay boys, so she just admires their feet and ignores the rest. And they are all reading books, worn paperbacks mainly, she imagines they've borrowed from roommates or girlfriends, or listening to their iPods on shuffle. Some of them are checking out the girls—their glamour-puss counterparts, equally casually yet strictly attired—looking at their asses or their hair or their new shoes, wondering what those shoes would look like wedged between bed and wall of their crappy, crumbly apartment, their naked bodies splayed out in some uncomfortable, pornographic position. They are wondering what it would be like to fuck them, Sarah Lee firmly believes. And while she doesn't want that, want them to only want to fuck her, she wishes, still, that they might glance at her. But they don't. They look anywhere but at her, in the old winter coat she bought at the ninety-nine-cents-a-pound Salvation Army outlet in Seattle, fading pink wool with childlike bejeweled buttons she sewed on herself, not as tough as it used to be, sometimes coats just die, she needs to admit that to herself one of these days; and even if they looked beyond the coat she knows she is too old and not cool enough for them, and sometimes she still speaks with a stutter when she meets new people (though it is much better now) so that even if they could see something in her, once she opened her mouth they might move on to the next person, pretend like she didn't exist, until suddenly, she simply didn't. And there is nothing worse than not existing.

So she takes the bus into the city instead, the B39 across the bridge, from the Southside of Williamsburg to the Lower East Side of Manhattan. She likes to think of her bus stops not by streets but by proper names, as if she were traveling from one kingdom to another, or at the very least, from one town to the next, so that she feels like she's really going somewhere very important, and not just across the bridge to work. On the bus, she is pretty again, a pretty thirty-two-year-old woman with nice waves of brown hair that go past her shoulders and cover her oversized ears (she has finally learned to cover them), and a full, healthy face, shiny like a silver dollar, with a smattering of freckles on her cheeks that make her look a little bit younger than she is, though not much. Enough to confuse the guy checking IDs at the door sometimes. She likes to think. She likes to believe.

The people who live in her neighborhood, she wouldn't consider them her neighbors. They, too, ignore her, won't meet her eyes as she walks down the block. She had tried greeting people the first month after she moved to the Williamsburg sublet, cheerful morning hellos that used to work sometimes in Queens, and in Oakland, and in Eugene, and in Portland before that, and in Seattle, too. No one wants to say hello to her, except maybe the deli guys who call her "Sweetheart" and "Mami," and serve her first when there's a long line, or the car-service drivers idling on the side streets who call out to her as she's walking. Sometimes she forces the Hassidic women working at the grocery store to interact with her, just so she can hear the sound of her own voice, asking them how they're doing, telling them to have a nice day. Are they timid or do they dislike her? She can't tell by their quiet responses, but she'll take them anyway.

On the bus she is surrounded by these so-called neighbors, the Dominicans from the projects, young women in sharp lip liner gabbing on cell phones while their children in tow suck quietly on hard candies, older women smoothing back their hair and sadly fingering the buttons on their coats, and young, agitated men who seem wired, pacing the aisles sometimes, checking pagers, waiting for information, waiting for something to soothe them.

Then there are the Hassidim, mostly men, they're allowed mobility more than their wives, she's noticed. They've got places to go, people to see, while the women seem to have children to raise, maybe some grocery shopping here and there, shuffling around the neighborhood, but it's the men who are free to fly throughout the city on short-term missions like homing pigeons, across the bridge and back again.

When Sarah sits behind them on the bus she stares at the backs of their heads, on occasion pulling out her sketch pad to draw them. She is mesmerized by the ruddiness of their skin, grubby stubble on the back of the neck and sometimes higher, how the folds of flesh (they are almost always overweight) bubbles over in layers on the collar of their shirt and jacket, like the lower part of her belly does onto her upper thighs after she has eaten too much pasta and drank too much wine. She has dozens of drawings like this, grainy black textures on heads of wavy pavement, all leading toward a stopping point, a block of black, the hat. Those thick black hats, conduits to their God, but also, she feels, protection from the world around them. They wear them to let everyone know they're in a posse, don't mess with them, because there are more, and they will take vengeance. Like gang colors, she mused. But there is only one color. Sometimes you only need one color.

3.

IT IS COLD. She blows on her hands to warm them, hugs her arms close around herself. She has been cold for days in her cursed sublet. There are three huge windows in the loft, and they face the East River, so early in the mornings and late at night the wind blows off the water and turns the apartment into a giant icebox. During the day it's better. There's sunlight, and it streams through the windows like a golden river.

4.

SARAH LEE goes where the sublets take her, she has for the last decade. Up and down the West Coast, starting in her undergraduate days at art school in Oregon, and then back up north to Seattle, down to Eugene, wherever she could find work, mostly as a seamstress, and a quick-and-easy furnished place to live. Everything she owns she could fit in a few boxes with the exception of her sewing machine and her sketchbooks and other artwork, much of which she still keeps in three storage units outside Portland. (Besides her cell phone, that's her only regular bill for

$387 a month. Everything else she pays up front.) She briefly lived with a man in Mendocino, a hearty crabber who had moved down from Alaska, for one lost summer of love, but when winter came and he headed back to work, he told her she'd need to move on or start picking up the rent herself. He'd be on his boat most of the time, and even though he'd be back on occasion, he didn't anticipate wanting to see her.

"I can't just have you staying here for no reason, can I?"

Why not? she thought. *Why can't you take care of me?*

Good for the summer, but not for the year. She'd heard it before.

She didn't mind this life at all, she liked the freedom, of course, but sometimes she thought about settling down in one place. She didn't even have a plant. She took care of other people's plants awfully well. Maybe if she had her own it would grow twenty feet high like in "Jack and the Beanstalk." If she had the time she could make things flourish. If she had the space.

But sublets were so simple. She didn't need to do a credit check, most of her moves were through word of mouth, so the references were covered, and she often didn't need to put a deposit down. The rent was never exorbitant—most folks just wanted someone who would take care of their stuff, their animals, their plants, their record collections, who would somehow even leave their house better than when they left it. Sarah sometimes stitched up tears in blankets, or sewed loose buttons back onto shirts or coats. She had hemmed a few curtains. Simple, easy fixes. Her references came easily. And then there was always someone who needed to sublet a new place. There was always someone on the go, waiting for a reliable young woman like Sarah Lee.

Use any of the spices you like. Just don't touch the liquor.

In Oakland Carter Michaelson tracked down Sarah Lee— he was always tracking her down, he'd been doing it for more than a decade—and asked her to come to New York for two months and watch his place. Carter was an old lover from art school who had made it big in New York with his vast, testosterone-infused sculptures that had people calling him the new Richard Serra, which was always funny to Sarah Lee, because the old Richard Serra was still around: Why did they need a new one? But Carter was irresistibly weird: He had a rolling mass of dark curls that stuck out like a thick bush around his head, matched with a plain, calm face, skin the color of a washed-out beach, and persistent blue eyes that popped out against his pale skin, all atop a set of gangling legs and arms. He looked like he should be famous, and therefore he was. It worked that way in the art world, that was always Sarah's understanding. Not that he needed any money: He had a trust fund that shot out a check for several hundred thousand dollars a year, some of which he blew on guitars and recording equipment for his rock band comprised entirely of aging artists, with the exception of the drummer, a recent art-school grad who kept the band full of weed and brought in young girls to their shows. Carter had a huge loft in Long Island City and two crazy dogs, a bulldog named Sasha and a lazy-eyed pit bull named Marcus. The pit bull hated practically everyone, but he loved Sarah Lee, which was why Carter was calling.

"I need you, Sarah Lee. You're the only one Marcus loves."

Carter was planning on going on walkabout in the Australian outback.

"I'm going to need at least two months," he said. "Maybe more. I need to be in a place where there are no buildings, just sky and land all around me. I need the absence of metal in order to contemplate it."

Whatever, it was a free place to stay.

On the night Sarah arrived in Queens, she slept with Carter, because she always slept with Carter when she saw him. He was just so *impressive* to her, even though she knew he was also full of shit, the way he mumbled and pretended not to understand people in order to dodge conflict, acted like he was in some sort of artistic space in public, isolating himself from the group, when he was really just stoned or bored most of the time. Or fucking with people, she knew he did that, too. He had admitted it to her before. She was his little sponge, soaking up his personality disorders, and they were legion.

But still, his was a compelling strangeness, and the sex was always so good. And she cared for him. And he for her. It was a twitchy kind of feeling she had when she saw him, like how her fingers felt after sewing for hours.

"Maybe you could stay longer, after I get back," he whispered in her ear. They were on his couch, naked, clothes everywhere, Sasha and Marcus sitting nearby with their tongues drooling from their mouths. "We could be a happy family."

She could not allow herself to take his offer seriously. She didn't want to be disappointed, and Carter had done it before. Yet she promised, "I'll think about it."

Her first week was spectacular: She took the dogs for long walks through the dirty but quiet streets of Long Island City, down past 5 Pointz, a massive compound of graffiti-strewn buildings that would send Sarah Lee into a creative frenzy for most of the afternoon. Plus she got an illustration gig with a weekly in town after getting drunk with an editor in an East Village dive. The editor loved her work, said she was just what New York needed, said she knew a creative director at an ad agency who would simply die over her stuff.

"*Die,* do you hear me?" The editor shook her shoulders. Such overzealousness always left Sarah Lee limp and distrustful, but it was affection, it was attention, and she needed it, so she let herself believe her a little bit.

But during week two, random women started showing up at odd times of the day and night, which is to say, at all times. One after the other: the stunning Asian woman in high-heeled leather boots who said she had left her book in Carter's apartment three weeks before, it was in the living room, it would just take a second, and yes, there it was, the collection of spanking stories that had made Sarah Lee blush when she flipped through it, but she was nice, so Sarah Lee had made her coffee and they had had a nice chat—her name was Mary, she hadn't known Carter was leaving town, no, no, it was nothing serious—until Marcus's growls drove her away; his studio assistant, Nina Sprout, in pigtails and a sweatshirt with the sleeves cut off, who stopped by to get her paycheck and was surprised to learn Carter had left town, who started to cry and freak out because how was she going to pay her goddamn rent, he hadn't said *word one* to her about this, it was just like a male artist, they think they own the fucking world because they have testicles, and then she suddenly stopped ranting when she opened her envelope and looked at her check, three months covered, "Have a nice vacation" written on the memo line, and Nina jumped up in the air and yelled, "I love testicles!"; and the blond German woman who hadn't needed to knock because she had keys and had crawled into bed next to Sarah Lee, and said, "Guess who's in town, darling?" and had wrapped her arm around her. Sarah Lee let her hold her for a second because it felt nice, and then she turned on the light and the woman screamed, just like they do in the movies, only it was real, it really fucking happened like that, it really did. The woman cursed her and Sarah yelled, "Wait, I'm just house-sitting," but it was too late, the woman was gone. And there were more bits and blips; Carter was constantly interrupting her life with his women even though he was thousands of miles away. Just think how it would be if he were here in town.

So Sarah knew she wouldn't be able to stay. But she wasn't ready to go back west, either. This editor seemed promising. And so when Carter returned from Australia, it was on to the next sublet.

5.

TODAY SHE'S taking the bus into the city to get some money together, money she desperately needs. She's been on rice and beans for weeks, and had barely scraped enough together to pay her phone bill and rent, just two bills and she couldn't even cover that. She shakes her head: thirty-two years old. Am I going to live this way forever?

But she was holding on, thinking that maybe this was the year she'd break through. Maybe today would be the day. You never know. At least she'll put a little money in her pocket— she'll pick up a few checks here and there, drop off some work, maybe get a coffee over near Tompkins Square Park, sit outside, not smoke any cigarettes, but just be around them for a little bit. Pretend like she's still there with the smokers, still part of the scene.

She stops first at Morris Juno's studio, a silk-scarf designer she sometimes assists with office work. He had called her a few days before and asked her to visit when she had time. She was hoping he was going to give her some sort of bonus check, that his holiday spirit spread straight through to January.

It seemed like she mostly got paid to be there and not talk; he was always telling her how much he liked her because she knew how to keep her mouth shut. Sarah Lee is used to being silent, a state she had cultivated initially because of her stutter, but had maintained even as she had progressed in life because she had so many things in her head to deal with first before she could speak. She has learned the lesson too many times that when she speaks too quickly it gets her into trouble.

"I don't know how you turned out this way, but god bless you," he had told her.

Morris lives on Rivington Street in a tenement with a depressing exterior—cigarette butts gathered on the front stoop like rain in a gutter and a paint job that had surrendered to the New York weather years ago—but the guts of the building were vibrant and alive, each floor housing a different artist who had knocked down walls and built in showers and archways and new doors, painted and nurtured and constructed, took the space and, like pioneers conquering new territories, carved out comfortable, rent-stabilized homes for themselves. (Sarah Lee was most impressed by the sense of permanence there, that people could do it, they could really stay put somewhere.) The tenants, all skilled carpenters and artists, were perfectly capable of transforming the front of the building, but they wanted to keep the place a secret, maintain the illusion of pregentrification for as long as possible.

"The minute they know you've got something good, they want it for themselves," said Morris. A short, hairy fireball of mysterious ethnic descent (some said Israeli, others Italian), he was obsessively protective of his personal space. He only took visitors from 10:00 to 11:00 AM daily, after his morning coffee, in his kitchen, unless you worked for him, in which case you were only allowed in his workspace—a spare bedroom off the living room he'd converted into a design studio—from 3:00 to 5:00 PM. If you came late to visit, you were not allowed in, and you were asked to leave promptly at 5:00, even if you were in the middle of something. But during his sample sales, he was a glorious host, and he had a reputation as a charming dinner companion and had a beautiful singing voice. He scoffed at the karaoke bars his friends tried to drag him to, but one or two bottles of wine into the evening, on the streets of Manhattan, if you linked arms with him and asked nicely, he would sing you love songs that would bring tears to your eyes. At least this is what Carter had reported to her before he left town. Morris had made Carter cry miserably, thinking of all the loves he had and lost in his thirty-four years, but then he felt free suddenly, and then full of something, love he supposed, and he had kissed Morris on the street.

"Not like that," said Carter.

"Sure," said Sarah.

"I'm not that way."

"Whatever you say, Carter."

"Sarah, I've made love to you a hundred times. You know that I'm a deeply feeling heterosexual man." He reached out toward her breasts. "Come here, let me feel you."

She let him feel her.

AT 10:30 AM Sarah buzzes Morris. Even though he kept hours from 10:00 to 11:00 AM, he really didn't want to see people until 10:30, and even then not till 10:45 AM. Fifteen minutes was just about all he could tolerate in the morning, but if he must, he must. You must, thinks Sarah. I need some money.

On the stairs, past orange walls and up to a skylight that welcomed sun up and down the interior, she finally lands in front of Morris's door. She knocks, and he opens the door slightly, just a wedge, peeks through, then, grudgingly, allows her in.

She tries not to take it personally. She understands the need for control. She tries to keep her mind at room temperature at all times.

He waves her in, a kiss on the cheek, and then a pinch on the other.

"I saw Carter the other day. He was asking about you. You should return his calls, I think. Don't be a silly girl."

Sarah hasn't been talking to him for weeks. She thinks she's mad at him, but she's not sure why. She thinks she might even hate him.

"Anyway, dear, enough of that. I asked you to stop by because I realized"—he says that last word as if he had made some great scientific discovery, a cure for cancer perhaps—"that I hadn't given you any sort of bonus for the work you did for me this holiday season. So I wanted you to have one of my scarves." He walks into his studio and returns with three scarves still in their plastic wrapping. "I think you need one of the fringed serapes.

These colors—" He splays them on the table in front of her: the first red with orange stripes, the next orange with brown stripes, and the third plum with pink stripes. "These colors will suit you."

Sarah Lee mentally calculates how much she might be able to get for the serape on eBay. A couple hundred at least.

"I like the plum for you, but you could do orange, too. Orange is such a happy color, and the plum, it might pull you down. It's up to you."

Well, it would be the plum, of course. Plum, somber but pretty plum. She moves her hand to the package, pulls it closer to her. But she's going to sell it anyway. She doesn't need a new scarf. It was frivolous. No one needs a silk scarf when you can buy a perfectly nice fleece one on St. Mark's for seven bucks, which is what Sarah had done. There was a time she might have coveted the scarves, but these days she just wanted to eat something beyond those rice and beans. She wanted steak, even if she wasn't dressed for it.

"Try it on, let me see it on you."

I bet I could get more for it if it's still in the packaging, thinks Sarah, but how could she insult him? It was a generous gift, more than she probably deserved for answering a few phones and ringing up credit-card charges. She rips open the plastic with her fingers and slips the scarf around her shoulders. And it was heaven. Of course. Her shoulders felt a warm pressure from the weight of the scarf, and when she rubbed her cheek against it, it was soft and comforting like the sound of someone's voice, a crooner singing a love song. She rises, walks to the mirror near the front door—the colors suit her perfectly, particularly the mood she's in today. There's the wine tint to her cheeks, as if someone had just pinched them, the gray in her green eyes, the auburn highlights in her hair, all swirling around next to this beautiful plum scarf. Her whole body is so warm now, everything about her feels more beautiful and spectacular.

She hears Morris in the background saying, "You should do nice things for yourself. You should take care of yourself. Little things. Like this."

No way in hell is this scarf going on eBay. She has to keep it. She is in love with this scarf.

6.

AFTER SHE leaves Morris, she walks up to Houston and hangs a right, then a left onto Avenue C, which will always feel like no man's land, no matter how many new condos they install. Years ago, when she still lived in Boston, people would tell her to stay away from Avenue C whenever she visited New York. She would visit with her high-school boyfriend, the one who got her pregnant, then weeks later ended up in jail for dealing drugs (Last she'd heard, he'd high-tailed it to Maine to avoid two separate sets of child support payments. A heartbreaker from start to finish). At the time, though, he was just a normal, totally fun stoner dude, and they would drive down on the weekends and stay with an aunt of his. She lived on the top floor of a town house in Chelsea with two gay men ("We're the sitcom of the future, you wait and see," one of the roommates said), and welcomed the youth of today with wide open arms and a glorious décolletage in full bloom. Sarah Lee loved to press up against her, what a joy it was. It made her boyfriend a little uncomfortable when he hugged his aunt, Sarah Lee could tell by the seriousness of his lips, straight and narrow and tight, but she was free to enjoy the embrace. She had read somewhere that people should get ten hugs a day, so she would take them when she could get them.

"That's your first problem right there," her boyfriend had said. "Reading articles. And your second problem is believing them." But he had hugged her all the time anyway, and secretly liked that Sarah Lee tried to understand the world around her in a different way than he did, which was usually through a cloud of pot smoke.

His aunt took club drugs in great quantities but never shared. However, she did tell them what part of the park to go to for dime bags if they had shown up empty-handed, and which bars were unlikely to card (all of them), and what parts of the city were safe. Avenue C wasn't on the list, neither was Avenue B for that matter, and Avenue A, barely.

"You two stay away from that park after dark," his aunt had said.

Today Avenue C had French restaurants, shops and galleries,

and, near the north end of it, one narrow storefront shop, Liberation, a legendary space (Carter used to see bands play there, swear to god, he told her. "How did they fit?" "They just did") that sold Sarah Lee's handmade Christmas cards, along with work from a handful of designers, the kind of stuff Sarah Lee sometimes thought of as art, and sometimes as useless crap: T-shirts screen-printed with outlines of birds or the faces of dictators, zines of poems or snapshots or personal tales of hard times on the road all hand-stapled or sometimes bound by a single extra-thick rubber band, and self-produced CDs made by noise bands from places like Portland and Chapel Hill and Chicago. (Sarah had picked up one of these once and discovered she had slept with the drummer from one of the bands and, blushing and horrified, had immediately shoved it to the bottom of the stack, as if that would prevent anyone from knowing the deep dark secret in her head.)

The owner of Liberation was a man named Travis James Crenshaw, but everyone just called him Doc because he was good with his hands. That's what he said anyway. It may have also had something to do with his stint as a prescription-drug dealer in the mid-'90s, but he went with the line that was more likely to make the ladies blush. He'd had the store for ten years, and had forty years left on his lease. Rent was five hundred dollars a month, and he slept in a cozy setup in the back of the store, about two hundred square feet, enough for a twin bed and small kitchen. So as long as he sold at least thirty dollars a day (minus what he paid to the artist, always fifty-fifty, that was his motto), and cooked all his own meals, Doc could keep up Liberation forever, or at least for the next forty years.

Plus he drank for free (or on the cheap anyway) at every East Village dive bar, so oftentimes he drank his dinner. The female bartenders in particular liked him because he was still handsome, with his dark eyes that flashed as if warning that he could cause trouble at any moment, balanced by a slender and crafted nose that made him seem important, a decision-maker, a leader. And he was gallant and polite, with a nice, warm southern voice he earned from eighteen years in Savannah, Georgia, as a youth. He would drag himself from bar to bar, around Tompkins Square Park, south of it mainly, Doc making the women smile, working the room. Sometimes Carter would join him— he liked making the rounds of lady bartenders as much as the next guy.

Sarah Lee went out with Doc once, right after the first time she met him. "It's a business meeting," he claimed. He was interested in selling some of her work in his store. But Sarah knew most business meetings don't happen at 9:00 PM on a Thursday, even if this was New York.

They went to a dive bar on the corner of 7th Street and Avenue B—"What's this place called?" "7B." "Right, of course."— and he proceeded to launch into a tirade about his ex-wife for the next hour. He used all kinds of awful words, obscenities flowed through his speech like champagne on New Year's Eve, only there was nothing to celebrate, just things to mourn, things to kick and stomp on, things to beat into the ground. His wife had left him for the man who owned the other gallery on Avenue C, the one that made more money, the one that got covered in *Art Forum* and the *New York Times,* the one that the man closed quietly, opening a larger space in Chelsea, taking Doc's wife with him. Chelsea is not that far away from the East Village, but Chelsea is a million miles away from Avenue C.

Put it to rest already, thought Sarah.

"I don't know why I'm talking this way," he said, and when he apologized later, it was clear he really didn't. But she was just sitting there so quietly, and she was new, she hadn't heard these stories before. It happened to her a lot. She was silent but seemed welcoming, warm, and she was attracted to the kind of people who needed to fill empty spaces with words; or perhaps, they were the kind of people who were attracted to her; or both, of course, both.

But the cursing, it just went on for far too long, and it made her feel that he might have that much venom for the next woman. She could be the next woman. But she didn't want to be next. She wanted to be last.

Eventually she simply got up and left—it was when he said "cunt"; she had no patience for that talk—and he walked outside after her, stopping to pat the door guy on the shoulder, no trouble here, mate, and then called her name; she was halfway down the block, walking toward Houston, she was always walking toward Houston, it seemed, when she was in the city, and she stopped.

He apologized again and again. "I'm just crazy," he said. "Please. Come back inside."

She declined.

"Then come by the store tomorrow. So I know that we're going to be friends."

And she did, because she woke up the next morning, thought it through, his heartbreak and his anger, and she wished that she could articulate it the way he did, not with the cursing, but the way he told the story in a straight line, the way each emotion was so real and vibrant to him. Maybe there was something to be learned from him, she didn't know what. She decided to be his friend.

So she brought the cards that she hadn't had a chance to show him the night before, and he spread them out before him on his desk and smiled at each one as he read them. Then she talked to him about a line of her own greeting cards; it wasn't high art, she knew, but people seemed to like her cards a lot when she sent them. She had done invitations for parties, too, baby showers and bachelorette parties, and everyone had always said, "You should have your own line," and that stuck with her, that she could have something of her own, because right now she didn't have very much of anything at all. But she had to be careful about where she put her work, she was protective of it at times, and she couldn't see her cards sitting in any old Hallmark store. They'd gather dust in the back if she wasn't careful.

A week later Doc sat for her for a sketch in his store, at a wide wooden table, animal claws for feet, and nicks on the top of it from a wild party where ladies danced on top of it in spiked heels—"You should have seen those girls dance." Doc took phone calls and rang up forty-five dollars' worth of sales and had something to say to practically everyone who walked in the door, knew them by first name, what they did, where they lived.

It was that first brisk fall day, and the wind had stung Sarah Lee's cheeks, surprising her, and people would just walk into the store to warm up for a while.

When the sketch was done, Doc loved it. She had drawn him with his mouth slightly open, an evil yet seductive grin, and he had three sets of hands, all in motion. She drew him younger than he actually was, but she thought he needed to be captured that way. Doc framed it and put it up on the wall behind the cash register, a proud demon shopkeeper.

He tells her all the time now that people try to buy his picture right off the wall, but he never sells it. "You could sell more," he tells her. "You could sit here on Saturdays and sell sketches for thirty bucks. People love shit like that."

She still contemplates it from time to time, but she wasn't sure if it would make her feel like one of those desperate failed artists trapped at Disney World, drawing caricatures of little girls with their favorite hobbies haunting the background. A tennis racket. A horse. A pretty blond doll with detachable parts.

AT LIBERATION, she finds Doc standing outside, smoking a cigarette. She asks him for a drag. He offers her a fresh one instead, and she accepts, feeling the cold brush off his arm onto hers where they meet for a moment. Then he lights another for himself, and the two of them stand outside in the cold for a while longer. The store is empty.

"Yeah, business has been bad since New Year's," says Doc. "Everyone's broke, even the people who shouldn't be broke, the rich kids in the condos. Or maybe they're just all shopped out." He motioned to a shiny new building down the street, where a doorman agonized behind a front desk. "No holiday spirit left. It's all in the toilet. With my business."

Sarah Lee looks at his stomach and waist to see if he has been eating, then looks into his eyes to see if he's sane. He needs to trim his nose hairs, she thinks, but besides that he seems all right.

"You all right?" she says.

He blusters like a teen boy, "Oh, I'm always all right, sugar, but thanks for caring," and for a moment Sarah Lee sees his younger self, a fresh young art-school student straight from the South, traveling the art world in the '80s in New York, death-defying feats of drugs and art and sex, twirling around like a ballet dancer, dazzling everyone around him.

"I'll take you at your word," she says.

"I owe you some money," he says. "And it's cold! Oh, sweet Jesus, it's cold. Let's get you inside."

He dashes into the backroom while she checks out his latest merchandise. She sees a new batch of screen-printed T-shirts; a new designer, she thinks, and she covets them. The design is intricate and original, no rip-off artist here, shiny silver paint shattered like a snowflake, each dot of paint like a small voice, on a sweet pink T-shirt cut and shredded and then resewn, so it hangs like gauze off the shoulders. It would look lovely on her, she thinks. She has good shoulders, the skin is soft and there are a few freckles. When she's alone sometimes she rubs her cheek against them and wonders if everyone's shoulders are this soft or if it is just hers. She checks the price tag—forty dollars.

Forty dollars. Two weeks of rice and beans with one vegetable a day; one happy hour with a friend, then a slice of pizza plus a cab ride home; her cell-phone bill; the haircut she gets once every three months from the cheapie Asian salon in the East Village that Carter introduced her to because he's in love with all the stylists; five packs of cigarettes; a year's supply of sketchbooks and ultrafine Sharpies. A steak dinner with one glass of cabernet. Forty dollars.

Doc emerges from the backroom, waving the check in the air, eyebrows raised like a vaudevillian comic. "You did all right this year, little miss." He hands it to her. It's for $305.00. She blushes. She can't even begin to extrapolate that number, she'll save the fantasizing for later when she's alone and wants to savor the day.

"We sold out of the cards," he says, then starts in on his next plan for her: Valentine's Day. They'd up the price this time because they could be presents as well as cards, he's sure he'd be able to get ten bucks a pop for something really special. He has plans for her and her little drawings, he says. Big plans.

"What do I know of love?" she says dramatically, and then she laughs, and he laughs, and there is briefly a moment of hysteria in the store, and then he says, "Exactly," and she knows she'll do it, she has twenty ideas at once. About love.

"I like this shirt," she says. "A lot."

"Yeah? It's mine. I mean I made it. I decided, why should you kids have all the fun?"

"It's beautiful, Doc."

"You should try it on."

"I couldn't. . . ."

"Try it on."

And so she goes to the backroom, his little hole in the wall with a few boxes of shirts and books and CDs and bookshelves and a spartan twin bed and a hot plate and a sink and a mini-fridge and she stops looking, shuts down after that, because the fridge is too much, it's so little, and she's sure there's nothing in there but a six-pack and a bottle of vodka anyway, maybe some mixers. Madly, she pulls off her sweater and pulls on the T-shirt, and then models it for Doc. He proclaims it perfect, it's as if he had been thinking of her the entire time, and she must have it, just take it, consider it a Christmas present.

"I have been waiting to do something nice for you since the day that I met you," he says, and there is an argument, a friendly one, and then finally he agrees to take twenty dollars for it. She pulls a twenty-dollar bill out of her wallet and hands it to him, and he takes it guiltily, but he is pleased, too—this is the first thing of his that he's sold in a long time.

"I think I'll wear it all day," she says. She shoves her sweater in her bag.

"You make me happy," he says, and he holds her hand for a second, and she lets him, because she still has a little holiday spirit left in her.

"Oh, fuck, I forgot to tell you," he says. "Carter's looking for you." And then, awkwardly, he drops her hand.

<hr>

7.

SARAH LEE crosses the park and heads west, toward Gareth's apartment. She is excited to see him more than anyone else today, because he is the nicest man she has ever met, and that includes every hippie in the Pacific Northwest and any man she has ever loved. Also he might be the one to change her life forever. They are trying to make a book together; he is writing it, and she is illustrating it. He is sort of famous and successful already—he is on NPR constantly, and has a children's book series about a giraffe named Camilla that is widely loved—but he wants to break into the adult market because he feels more like an adult now than he has in years, that's what he told her. He is married, he has a baby on the way, and he has bought an apartment. He is almost grown.

"I have shed my twenties completely," he has said. "A layer of useless skin I'd like to forget."

At Gareth's house the buzzer doesn't work. She presses it for a minute straight, and there's no response. A pile of errant snow, dirty from the streets, forgotten by plows and last weekend's sunshine, lies near a garbage can, and Sarah Lee packs together a snowball, hurls it at his window, nails it. After a moment, Gareth comes to the window, flakes and water dripping down it, looks at the street and waves at Sarah, then mouths, "I'll be right down," and then, just to make sure she understands, points downward.

"Yes, yes." Sarah nods, and then laughs.

Gareth hustles to the front door, out of breath. He reaches to his cowlick, neatens it, and it flops down again on his forehead. Sarah Lee has often wanted to press it in place herself, but she has resisted. He is not hers to touch.

He rests on the door for a moment, this large man, a boisterous king of a man, whose flesh is simultaneously solid and unyielding like the wall of a castle, and soft and embraceable, something to sink into for comfort. Sarah Lee can't picture him as a smaller man; she hopes that he stays big forever. It is nice to know in a city of wasted-away youth that a man like Gareth exists.

He pushes the door open with his free hand, in the other there is a baby monitor. He hugs Sarah, and she allows herself the pleasure of it for a moment.

"Sarah Lee, my dear sweet girl," he says. "I'm so delighted. Company, at last!"

They take the three flights slowly, the stairs ache with each step.

"Laura's home now," he tells her. "In bed. The doctor made her. 'Stay in bed,' he said, and so there she is. In bed."

"Is she OK?"

"Well, yes. And no. She's having trouble breathing. She's so petite, you know, and she's carrying everything up front. All that weight on such a delicate woman, it's remarkable. She's never weighed that much before. But the baby is fine."

They stop outside his front door. The Christmas wreath is still hanging, two birds with holly in their mouths, entwined in straw and yarn.

"They think the baby should be fine," he says. "Everything is supposed to be fine."

"It's going to be fine," she says. She hugs him again, and this time lets him hold on to her.

"Of course it is," he says. "And then she was driving me mad with all the yelling back and forth from her room to the kitchen, so I got these." He waves the baby monitor. "We needed them anyway."

They are still standing in the hallway and time is passing very slowly, like the time before someone kisses you for the first time, thinks Sarah, only this is not about a kiss. A forceful wave of emotion plunges into her, and she feels dizzy. It isn't about her, it isn't her moment, but she is still a servant to her surroundings. And then she remembers to focus, and she is back, she is present again.

"I don't want to go back in there," says Gareth. He looks down sadly, embarrassed. His ears flush pink, and Sarah wants to grab them to see if they're as warm as she thinks they are.

"It's OK to feel that way," says Sarah.

"Things have been . . . difficult," he says.

"You can handle it," she says. And then, even though she didn't know if it was true, even though she had only known him a few months, she chucks his shoulders with her hands and boldly tells him, "This is the moment you've been waiting for your entire life."

"Well, I don't know if it was this *exact* moment," he says.

"No, it was this one. I checked," she says drily. She laughs at him, and then he starts laughing, too, and then the moment is over, and everything she felt drains from her body. Relief. At last.

THE BOOK they are making is about rats beneath the city and lovers aboveground, all living off the same alley in New York. Some panels are split in half, others in quarters, so multiple story lines are visible at the same time. There are some characters who are identifiable only by their shoes, and others by their tails. There is a heroine, and her name is Mirabella. She looks like Gareth's wife, Laura. To a T. Tiny bones, olive skin, dark black hair like a shroud. There is a young man, Ali, who rides a skateboard around town, and he's in love with a woman named Amy who wears pink high heels and clips made of shiny pearls in her hair, and an older man, Horace, who has sturdy brown boots with laces and makes sure all of the animals in the city are fed, and is sometimes watched by a mysterious woman who lives behind purple curtains. And there are rats named after saints, like Luke and Agnes and Antonia, some with longer story lines, pairing off and traveling together, and some that make only brief appearances, spouting off one-liners, truisms of life. All of the characters have the same mission: They are all marching desperately through this alley, trying to fall in love.

They haven't decided on a title for it yet. Sarah likes *Love Alley* but Gareth thinks that sounds like a porn title. "Like ladies of the evening in the red-light district of Amsterdam." It sounds romantic when he says it like that, thinks Sarah, but he makes everything sound romantic.

They have spread out the new pages Sarah Lee brought on his kitchen table, salt and pepper shakers and electricity bills shoved aside, the baby monitor holding down an errant corner of a page. The sketches are in black and white, and the table is vintage 1950s style, with peach-and-blue swirls decorating the square top lined with silver. They are sitting on matching peach vinyl chairs that squeak slightly as they move. Gareth has made fresh coffee and brownies. The brownies have walnuts in them. They are still warm. Sarah Lee is trying not to get crumbs on her sketches, or on her new shirt, or on her new scarf. This is why I don't bother dressing this way, she thinks. It's too much work.

Occasionally the baby monitor spurts and fits, Laura in the other room sighing, breathing, shifting. Twice Gareth has to leave the table, first to refill her water pitcher, and once for an unexplained reason; she just called—"Gareth, I hate to interrupt your meeting, but . . ."—and he rushed off to the bedroom, stayed for a few minutes, and then came back smiling, shaking his head.

"What a sense of humor that woman has," he says.

"What does she do all day in there?"

"Reads to the baby. Reads to herself. Watches television. Hates her life while trying not to hate the baby." Gareth smoothes one edge of a sketch. "I play a lot of cards with her. She's quite good. I'm inclined to send her to Vegas after the baby is born. The college fund needs a little padding."

"I can't imagine sitting still all day long," says Sarah.

"She's hanging in there," says Gareth. "She's simply remarkable. The love of my life, you know. I don't know what I would have done if I hadn't met her. I dated so many crazy women in New York, I was starting to turn crazy myself. The smart ones are always a little crazy," he says, and winks. "And then, there she was, in the midst of all these sad and miserable and just—*confused* people, there was my Laura, sane and joyful with a voice and mind as clear as a bell."

The baby monitor emits a thick cough, and then a long wheeze.

"And she was funny and beautiful and she liked the same books, the same music, and she wanted everything I did, was in the exact same place I was in life, and just like that, add water and mix, instant love."

These are the things we do sometimes, she thinks. We

remind ourselves of why we're in love, so that we can stay that way. It's not a permanent state, remember that, she tells herself.

"You're lucky," says Sarah. She is warmed by Gareth's effusion, but sometimes another's excess of love reminds her of her absence. She is all alone in the world, she thinks.

"Oh, please, my dear. Everyone is in love with you!" He shoots it out of his mouth and starts to laugh, it's a short noise, then gets her more coffee, makes her take another brownie, won't take no for an answer, he made them especially for her, after all. The baby monitor whirrs, Sarah Lee makes a note on one of the sketches, and the room is suddenly full of air again. Gareth has two months left until his life is changed forever, for the better, she knows it, and Sarah Lee wonders how long it will take until that moment arrives for her.

"By the way," says Gareth later, as Sarah Lee bundles herself up to leave. "I believe Mr. Carter Michaelson seeks an audience with you."

"So I hear," she says.

"It seems inappropriate for me to tell you what to do," says Gareth. He sucks in his breath, the wall of his body rising high. A buttress. "I don't like to get in other people's business."

Sarah concentrates on the bejeweled buttons of her coat.

He exhales, inch by inch, the wall collapses. "But you should call him," he says. "Because he loves you."

Love.

8.

SHE STOPS ON the front stoop of Gareth's apartment build-ing, she sits, she takes out her cell phone, she puts the cell phone away, she gets up, dusts off the back of her coat, walks to Avenue A, turns right, walks to the café where she orders a cup of coffee to go, asking them to leave room for milk.

In the cup of coffee she empties one packet of sugar, deli-cately shaking it so no granule is wasted. Then she pours milk into it, fills it up to the top of the cardboard cup, until the coffee is cooled. She takes a sip. She pours more milk. She repeats the process. Now it is perfect.

The café is full, so she walks to the park, past the cops lin-gering near the front entrance and the nannies with their charges in the playground and the junkies haunting the benches and the indie kids taking pictures of the dead trees in the winter with their digital cameras. She sits in the center of the park on the wide half moon of benches that surround an island of trees that poke up through the concrete. A committed hippie rides by on his bicycle. A slender man with high cheekbones in a long swing-ing fur coat walks two West Highland terriers. The dogs are adorable. Sarah Lee makes a kissing sound at them, and one turns toward her, ears pert.

It is still early in the day, but it seems late. The sun will set soon, the sky is already graying, the blues of it sucked away like water down a drain. She thinks of the noise a drain makes as it sucks in the last bit of water. It is vaguely satisfying. She is vaguely satisfied; in fact she is on the cusp of complete satisfaction, she teeters there, undecided. To give into complete satisfaction is to allow that it can disappear as quickly as it arrived. Once you feel it, you will want it forever. And you cannot have it forever. Because life is not perfect.

9.

HE ANSWERS on the first ring.

"Stop telling people you love me," she says, and she starts to cry, tears so rich with salt her cheeks sting on impact.

"But I do love you," he says.

"Here is what I want," she says. "I want you to stop fucking other women. If you leave town, I want you to take me with you. If we go to a party, I want you to stay by my side until I feel comfortable being by myself. And tonight I want you to buy me a steak dinner because I am so fucking sick of eating rice and beans."

"Yes," says Carter. "I can do that. Where are you? I will come and find you right now, and we will go and eat steak."

"I'm in Tompkins Square Park."

"I'll be there in twenty minutes. I love you. I'm going to kiss you as soon as I see you."

"OK."

She hangs up her cell. The next kiss I get will be the best one of my entire life, she thinks. It will never be better than this moment. But I will have it, I will have this moment. It will be mine.

10.

IT IS NIGHT NOW, and Sarah Lee sits and waits for love.

Acknowledgments

PORTIONS OF THIS BOOK appeared in *Pindeldy-boz* ("The Perfect Triangle") and *Bullfight Review* ("Instant Love"). "He Gives Pause" was originally released as a zine, and I thank Joni Rentz and Dave Savage for their visual contributions to it.

I also enthusiastically thank: Josh Abraham, Sarah Balcomb, and Paul McLeary for their thoughtful readings of early and late drafts; Bernie Boscoe and John Levenstein for their generous provision of the time and space to write; Megan Lynch and Whitney Pastorek for their enthusiasm and support; Cinde Boutwell and Kerri Mahoney for putting up with all my crap; Doug Stewart for guiding me through this process with such care; and Sally Kim for her exceptional patience and wisdom.

As always, love to my family.

About the Author

JAMI ATTENBERG'S work has appeared in Salon, *Nylon, Print, Pindeldyboz,* the *San Francisco Chronicle,* and *Time Out New York.* She lives in Brooklyn, New York. Visit her at jamiattenberg.com.

About the Type

THIS BOOK was set in Adobe Garamond, a typeface designed by Robert Slimbach in 1989. It is based on Claude Garamond's sixteenth-century type samples found at the Plantin-Moretus Museum in Antwerp, Belgium.

Composition by Stratford Publishing Services
Brattleboro, Vermont

Printing and binding by Berryville Graphics
Berryville, Virginia